When
Comes

David F Pennant

Silver Lining Books
Woking

By the Same Author

The Priorities of Jesus

The Piano Teacher (trilogy)
The Inventor's Folly (sequel)
The Investigator's Choice (conclusion)

The Garden of the Galaxy
36 Days in Intensive Care
Earthquake Tremors
Follow Jesus!

www.pennantpublishing.co.uk

Prologue

Pray that it will not be winter when that time comes
(Matt. 24:20)

-oOo-

When the moment arrived, it was still a surprise, despite all the preparation. Just a brief shout from the hall, "They're coming!", although it was hardly necessary as I had already heard some distant shots from down the road.

I quickly began to peel off my short-sleeved sweater and unbutton my shirt. Trousers and socks went next; would I ever need them again? There, now I was naked apart from my underpants. Their brilliant whiteness would show that we had not let standards slip here.

People stepped aside so I could pass. Everyone was looking very tense as I opened the front door, and no wonder. But there was nothing more to be said. I had given all the advice I could in case I did not come back.

Saying goodbye to Mark had been surprisingly hard. He might look tough and independent, aged twenty-five and six foot three, but he was still my boy inside. There were tears in his eyes after we had finished a long hug.

I suddenly recalled his first attempts at riding a bicycle on the field just a few miles from this house, aged four; me shoving him forward, him pedalling for all he was worth and crashing over painfully after just a few yards. Then we would do it all over again. My knees used to feel so sore, in sympathy! Still, he never gave up until he had mastered it.

I strode briskly across the forecourt, under the fine acacia tree and out onto the middle of the road. Our side of it had detached houses, four bedrooms each, and the far side comprised pairs of three bed semis. A typical suburban road. Thank goodness it was a sunny day in May. It did not feel cold at all; it was about midday. Standing in the middle of the road no longer felt strange – it was an age since we had seen a car pass.

The slight bend in the road was an advantage, as it meant that the approaching crowd would not see me until they were a hundred yards away, and by that time there could be no mistaking me for what I was; an unarmed man as good as naked. The important thing was not to show my nervousness.

My eye fell on the cherry trees spread out at intervals in the middle of the wide grass verge on the far side of the road. The blossom had been magnificent this year, but even the last petals had disappeared from the side of the road by now. To think that the council used to spend money clearing it all up, when the wind did it just as effectively if you left well alone.

The planners had done well with this tree-lined road, I thought. It made for a pleasant entry to the town from the East, and the weight restriction keeping heavy lorries away had helped to make it a pleasant road to live in. We too had done well recently in keeping the grass neatly manicured with the pre-war hand-pushed mower which we had found in Reg's shed.

There was a burst of machine gun fire from the advancing crowd, rat-tat-tat-tat. It was much closer now. It was so hard not to tremble.

I had a horrible thought. Had I been wise to keep my sandals on? No, surely not. It had been a mistake! It would give a counter message, that I was prepared to run if necessary. I ought to have been in bare feet. How incredibly foolish! I should have made myself one hundred percent vulnerable, not ninety-nine. That poor decision could cost me my life.

I broke out into a sweat. Keep calm, and carry on with the plan. None of the windows in the houses had any faces looking out; well done, everybody. Face the armed gang head on. Put the hands up slowly, palms forward, in the traditional pose. If only the fingers would keep from shaking!

There were shouts; I had been spotted. I avoided eye contact, as I had learned when a teenager that if you meet a tiger in the jungle, you should not look it in the eyes, because tigers interpret eye-contact as aggression. The crowd was twenty or thirty strong, I guessed, and they appeared to have a mortar. No wonder they felt confident, marching forward boldly into a strange town.

"It's a trap," yelled somebody, and barrels were aimed at me. I braced myself. It was now or never.

Chapter One

I suppose it's easy to say it now with hindsight, but I did actually know there was something wrong when I woke on that fateful Tuesday morning.

It was not so much the power cut – the display on our digital clock on my side of the bed was blank, but the sound of the world that was wrong. I could hear the birds in the garden distinctly. They should have been drowned out by the passing traffic. Why wasn't there any?

It was ridiculous of people to say that the birds were dying out. If you were awake at dawn, which I had been quite often in the months after Sonia died, they were very much in evidence. The early morning concerto rivalled anything by Handel or Bach.

I had overslept a little, which was unlike me. Normally I wake a few minutes before the alarm goes off. I would need to be prompt if I was going to catch my usual train into London.

I crossed the landing to the bathroom, pausing to greet Timber our Golden Retriever lying on her bean bag as I passed. She was barely awake and did not even lift her head.

The water pressure was low when I brushed my teeth, which was odd.

I dressed quickly. It still felt strange not having Sonia. However long would it take before it felt normal being single again, I wondered for the fifteenth time.

I gave Timber her breakfast and had my usual bowl of cereal and milk. I was careful to close the door of the fridge quickly to conserve the cold. I somehow sensed that this power cut was likely to last a while even then.

I needed information. We had a portable radio somewhere, and there might be the correct batteries in the batteries box, I reflected. I soon located the radio, but it needed six batteries and the old shoe box we used to store odd batteries only had two, left over from the multiple packs that you seemed to have to buy these days when you simply wanted one battery. I doubted whether I could scrounge enough batteries by robbing other appliances round the house to make up the number. How tiresome. Never mind.

Soon I was ready to leave for work. I had lost all interest in my high-powered job in the city when Sonia died, ringing New York and Tokyo three or four times a morning, but I needed to keep at it to pay the bills and get Mark and Fliss through university. It was rather embarrassing having everybody tell me how good at it I was. I could have done it standing on my head if the truth was told. My policy with remarks of that kind was simply to smile sweetly and carry on. But surely there must be more to life than this?

I settled Timber with a chocolate drop, grasped my briefcase and opened the front door. The road was deserted. There wasn't a single car, and even more surprising, no pedestrians either. I stood still and stared. Also, where were the trains? The railway line to London was two hundred yards beyond the far side of the road, but as it was raised up on an embankment the noise of trains tended to carry in our direction with the prevailing wind. You could also see the frequent trains in gaps between the houses. It should have been busy at this time, but today the track was standing eerily idle.

This might be Tuesday, but it felt like Sunday.

I think it was then that I first started to feel scared. What would Sonia do? She would know...

I looked next door. We were on good terms with Phil and Kath our next door neighbours. They left for work about now in the normal way, but both cars were still on the forecourt. The doorbell was a battery-powered one, and gave a friendly chime. Phil and Kath both came to the door.

"What's going on?" I asked.

"We haven't a clue," said Kath. They were younger than us, not yet ready to think about retirement.

"There are no trains and no cars," I said.

"And no planes," Phil added. "Haven't you noticed?"

"No." The airport was about twenty miles away, and although the planes often came over us, they were too high to hear. The sky had none of the usual tell-tale exhaust plumes. I had no doubt Phil was right.

"Have you heard anything on the radio?" I enquired. "I don't have the right batteries."

"We haven't tried. My laptop is down," Kath declared. "Or rather, all I get from it is a flashing cursor."

It is strange how slow I am to catch onto the new technology, really. Although I use the internet all day at work, my mind still does not jump to it as a source of news.

"Also, our phone line is dead and my mobile is not working," Phil added. "It's very unusual for a power cut to affect the phone."

"I've got a bad feeling about this," I said. "It's clear there's no getting to work today. I would like to call a Neighbourhood Watch meeting to compare notes and make a plan. Shall we say at 1030?"

"Well, alright." Kath seemed somewhat taken aback. "We are working at home today in any case. Do you think it's serious?"

"Yes, I think it's serious. Look, can you tell the houses this way," I pointed away from the town centre on our side of the road, "and I'll do the ones the other way and on the other side. We are all going to need each other, I reckon."

They agreed. "Right. See you later."

I made my way up and down the road knocking on doors. Everybody was in and just as mystified as I was. None of them had been able to contact the outside world. They seemed relieved that somebody was doing something and agreed to come to the meeting. It was a good thing we had a large conservatory joined on to our kitchen, I reflected, although it was still going to be a squeeze.

Sonia would not have enjoyed the invasion, I reflected. That was partly why I had never convened a Neighbourhood Watch meeting until now. She liked to keep the home to ourselves as a refuge from the world. Although I always maintained that I would have liked to keep an open house, the reality was that although I was now free to invite others in at all hours, I still carried on in the same manner of life as when Sonia was here. It was as if I had lost the will. There were some days when I wondered if I was suffering from depression, but the thing to do was to shrug it off and to carry on.

Then there was also Pamela...

Chapter Two

I was just finishing some unaccustomed bread and marmalade when I heard a key turning in the lock of our front door. This was very threatening. I crossed the hall in record time, wondering what was happening.

"Valerie!" I exclaimed as the door opened. I had totally forgotten that Tuesday morning meant the house being cleaned. I don't see Valerie from one moon to the next as I'm normally on the train.

"Come in."

"It's very quiet out there," Valerie remarked. "Hardly a soul about. Rather nice really."

Was it as simple as that? Was I being paranoid imagining the worst? It must be nice to have a straightforward outlook on life, like Valerie's. Not that her life was simple as a mother of two lively youngsters, far from it, but that was none of my business.

"Well, I think there's something funny going on, but never mind, we'll find out sooner or later. How's the family?"

"They're fine. Susan got a special commendation at school last week."

"Sounds wonderful. I don't think I ever got one of those."

We both laughed as Valerie began to get her cleaning things out of the cupboard under the stairs.

"Donald is to have some tests for his skin condition on Thursday."

"I hope they will go well and get to the root of the problem."

"The trouble is, they involve a needle and he's scared of injections."

"I don't blame him. Who wants to be punctured like a pin cushion?"

Then I paused.

"Valerie, I'm sorry if I seem rather distracted today, but my brain is taken up with what's going on outside, or rather what's not happening. Haven't you noticed the absence of cars and trains?"

"It's only a power cut, and the trains are affected, so people are staying put. Don't you think..?" Valerie suddenly sounded concerned.

"Well, the phones are off, mobiles too, and next door's laptop computer has malfunctioned and there are no planes in the sky, so no, I think there's something bad going on. If I was you, I would abandon the cleaning and get your children home from school. We've called a Neighbourhood Watch meeting here at 1030 to pool ideas. I suggest you do the same for the people in your area."

"Oh!" Valerie fell silent, deep in thought. "My husband is at home, and the children can make their own way back if they need to. It's only half a mile for them. No, if I may, I'd like to whisk round quickly with the duster and then stay to your meeting and hear what people think. Then I'll make my way."

"Alright." This was surprising, but why not?

"Anyway, have you any suggestions as to how to deal with Donald's fear of needles?"

I tried to concentrate on our conversation, but my mind was racing. Suddenly, a horrible suspicion formed itself. It's not so much that I thought of it – it just came on its own.

"What's the matter?" Valerie's voice was concerned. I dragged myself back to the present.

"Sorry. I think I know what's happening and it's not pretty. Ah, here are the first people." The loud knock on the front door was unmistakeable. "They're very early. We'd better leave cleaning there for today."

"Okay." Valerie was handing me back the money for the cleaning, which I had put out in cash when I realised who it was that had come. I hesitated. It was tempting to take it.

"Look," I said, trying to keep the concern out of my voice, "I think you had better hang on to that. You may need it." Then I had an inspired afterthought. "You can pay me back next week if I turn out to be wrong!"

Valerie was looking really worried by now, but there was no time for more as I needed to answer the door. They were very early; it had only just gone ten.

Virtually the whole of our end of the road entered in one go. I thought it would never end. Timber soon gave up barking and retreated upstairs. Ah yes, and here was Pamela, with a spring in her step. So she had come. Distractingly pretty! I muttered something in greeting. Why she was single I couldn't understand.

I ushered them all through to the conservatory. On sunny days like today, the temperature tended to soar by the afternoon, even in Spring, but it was not too hot in there yet. It was a bit chilly still to think of spilling out into the garden.

"All I can offer you is a glass of water," I apologised, as I fetched glasses from a wall unit. The water pressure was certainly low; there was no denying it. The question was, was it getting feebler or was it holding up? The glass of water would help me at any rate. My grasp of the situation was developing by the minute. I was wondering whether I was going to be sick.

Then a new thought entered my mind. Why was I so slow?

"Excuse me a moment," I said, and made my way upstairs and into Mark's bedroom. He was not pleased at being woken, but I told him it was important and he had a right to be present at the meeting. He said he would be down in a few minutes.

Chapter Three

When everyone was settled, I called the room to order.

"Look, I feel the need to start with an apology. The fact is that despite being Neighbourhood Watch Co-ordinator for this end of Standish Road, I only know about five of you by name. I only became the Co-ordinator because nobody else was willing to do it. All I do is put round a news sheet two or three times a year, and send out an email if there is anything that needs to be communicated. I suppose the lack of contact is because we have had so few problems in our road.

"This is the first meeting we have ever held. You are all very welcome. Better late than never."

There were some non-committal nods and grunts. I continued.

"We are all aware of the power cut and the drop in water pressure and lack of transport."

"Sorry," said a man I did not know, "did you say lower water pressure?"

For answer I turned on the kitchen tap. A number of people nodded, agreeing with my assessment.

"But there isn't any connection, surely?" the man persisted.

Kath from next door broke in. "Our computers are not just down, they are dead, and the phones are useless. Our two mobiles are both dis. Do you reckon all that occurring at the same time is coincidence?"

"I don't see how it can all be connected."

This man was not one to give up easily.

"Sorry, I don't know your name," I said.

"Greg Mitchell, married to Myra here. We only moved in a few weeks ago." Myra smiled weakly. Greg was clearly the leader in their relationship.

"I'm Matthew Price, and this is my son Mark just coming in. Right, Greg and all of you, this is not going to be easy." I gulped. "I think I know what is going on. Two or three years ago, I happened to catch part of a programme on TV about the solar system, which explained in passing that in theory, the sun could have a hiccough or something like that and send out rays which could affect communications on earth." I was trying to break it gently. "Well, more than just affect them. It seems that in certain circumstances, a freak burst of radiation could hit us which would ruin the microchips that we all depend on."

From the blank faces, it was evident that I would have to spell things out more clearly.

"Look, all these hand-held devices that we have grown so used to have electronic wizardry running them, created by very clever people. The central part is a tiny computer chip made of silicon, covered with minute printed circuits. My fear is that there has been one of these flares on the sun's surface, and it has knocked out these chips, rendering all our computerised devices useless."

"Well, so what?" queried Pamela.

"Wouldn't we have noticed if there had been a flare?" someone else put in.

"Not necessarily. Radiation lands on us all the time. Apparently, each of us is bombarded by billions of Neutrinos every second. They are so small that they can go through the earth without hitting a single molecule on the way. I read popular science books for relaxation in case you're wondering. Anyway, I don't know what particular rays would be damaging for computer chips, but suppose there has been a surge, all the computers in Europe could be useless. So the power cut, rather than causing the problem, is just one of the results of the flare. Everything is so dependent on computers that I guess the grid would just shut down if the computers stopped functioning."

"Aren't you forgetting about the backup systems Matthew," Phil interposed. "Nobody would be so foolish as to neglect proper rigorous procedures to keep the power running."

"But Phil, don't you see, all these systems use electronic wizardry, backups included, and these days that means computer chips. That's why there are no planes; they all have computers on board. Same with the trains and the phone networks."

There was a sudden buzz of conversation as each person turned to their neighbour, which was soon broken by an Italian lady sitting opposite.

"*Non comprendi, non comprendi. Ees problemmo?*"

I do not speak Italian, but even I could manage a reply. "Yes, yes, *problemmo, problemmo grande. Grande, grande, grande!*" Not for the first time I wondered why we had an Italian community in our road, and why they had made so little effort to integrate with the rest of us. Then it occurred to me that perhaps there had been little attempt to show

17

friendliness on our part and that they were hardly to blame.

I had an idea.

"Look, how many of you have tried to start your cars?"

"I did," said Georgina, a retired lady from three doors up much given to frequenting art galleries, "but I had a flat battery. I was rather surprised."

"You see, modern cars have computer chips under the bonnet. I suggest a few of us try our cars and then gather back here again."

It took several minutes, but it was soon clear that nobody was getting a response. Our own car was typical; although the central door-locking functioned properly, there was not even a click when I turned the key in the ignition. That would be the immobiliser being unable to communicate with the electronics, I reckoned. However, at least the remote unlocking worked on the cars; presumably infra red devices would be unaffected.

While I was doing the checks an idea came to me.

When the people were assembled again, I said "I have a suggestion which will help make things clear. If one of us has an older portable radio, that is an analogue instrument which has medium and long wave bands on it, not one of these modern digital ones with one-touch tuning, then we can try for radio stations not just in the UK but also overseas as well."

"We have a 1960s radio with a rotating dial for tuning," said Greg. "My father died recently, and when we were clearing out his house I saved it from the dump because I remembered us using it when I was a child. I think it still works. I'll go and get it."

"Excellent. Couldn't be better. Thanks."

It took ten minutes to get the right batteries and power it up. It produced a pleasing hiss.

"Right, Greg, try the long wave."

Greg was already rotating the dial with a worried face. There was nothing except the steady hiss. He made his way slowly through the dial and then back again. As he did so, the sound changed. The hiss died away to a silence, and then a clear voice announced, "This is Max Phillips broadcasting from Hindhead in Surrey. Is anybody there? Over."

I clapped my hands in glee. "Wonderful. That will be an amateur radio ham, with a diesel generator powering thirty year old equipment probably. We had a set up like that when I was at school; second world war equipment, I reckoned. I inherited a key to the little room as head of signals in the School Corps. I used to listen to the chatter on the big old set, but I never dared send anything. Of course, we can't reply, but somebody might. Note the frequency, Greg."

It was while we were searching the other bands to no avail that Phil said, "We need to repeat this exercise at the most promising times of day, to my mind, on the hour for example. This Max Phillips could turn out to be a source of news."

"Good notion," I said.

I could see that the people in the room were divided. Some were with me; others were sceptical, but most were simply bemused. Too bad. I had done my best. It was time to press on.

19

"So, if the phone people manage to get the exchanges to work, which I doubt, then your only chance of being able to make a call is if you have a pre-digital instrument, in other word one of the old ones with a dial. And to be blunt, you can forget about your mobile phones. I'm afraid these hand held things we have all grown so used to, and the masts and the exchanges are not going to work again. You might as well put them in a drawer."

"The young people are going to be lost without their mobiles," Mark broke in.

His tone was resentful and aggressive. I felt a sudden surge of anger.

"Look, we have far more serious problems to worry about than young people wasting their time texting each other with trivia!"

I should not have spoken in that tone. I immediately regretted it. In reply Mark stood up knocking his chair over in the process, unlocked the back door and stormed out. I caught Pamela's eye, and wilted at her expression. Okay so I was feeling stressed, but did I really need to take it out on my son?

I felt a deep sense of dismay.

Chapter Four

"Does the gas work?" somebody asked.

I moved across the room and turned on a gas ring, and there was silence. "No," I said, turning it off again.

"Right, there's a lot more to say, but I think we need to be practical," I announced. "The decreased water pressure is bothering me. My advice is that you all go back home and do two things; turn off the gas at the main stopcock, to save possible explosions if by any chance they do manage to put the gas back on, and also to fill up all the screw-top bottles you have with tap water for drinking later. I don't know whether the water is going to fail altogether or not. It would have been sensible to design our system of mains water pipes so that all homes are gravity fed, but I'm willing to bet that electricity is required for pumping, and that there are microchips in the electric circuits."

"Actually, there's a move to take out the old water towers on stilts because people find them unsightly," a man in a dark suit called out as he was rising to his feet. I might have guessed!

People were getting up to go.

"No wait, please don't go yet. It so happens that I collect the coloured screw tops that come on plastic milk bottles for charity, and I have fifty or so in a bag here, so it's worth rummaging in your recycling bin for plastic bottles even if you've thrown out the top. When you know how many tops you need, please come back and ask."

People were getting up to leave.

"Oh, one more thing. I don't think we should use our loos. The water is too precious. Go in the garden if you need to. We will hold another meeting here at eight this evening."

My suggestion about using the garden as a toilet had caused consternation.

"Isn't that a health risk?" asked Greg.

"Well, I don't want to frighten you, but does anyone know what happens to the sewage after it reaches the sewer?"

Everybody looked blank. A few heads shook from side to side.

"I thought not. Well, suppose the sewage farms have back-up generators alright, but their electronic systems are microchip-controlled and stop operating and everything grinds to a halt, then we could find the sewers filling up, and then we would have a real health problem. No, it's better to go in the garden to be on the safe side."

That had them really worried. They had had enough. They surged out of the house. One lady vomited in the flower bed outside the front door and hurried off without stopping to apologise. Great!

Phil, Kath and Greg had remained behind, and Valerie was hovering in the background, wanting to leave but having something to say.

"Valerie?" I enquired.

"You were magnificent in there; I knew you would be. I will go and spread the word to our neighbours about what to do. May I come back at eight?"

"Of course. Bye."

"How come you are so sure of everything?" Phil asked. "It's almost as if you were prepared." Phil's tone had a slightly aggressive tone to it, I felt. Had I said something to upset him?

"Look," I said defensively, "it's only because I came across a book called *The Long Emergency*. The author was envisaging the collapse of society in America when the oil price goes through the roof. He went into considerable detail. It's the only book I have read six times in a row; I found I needed to in order to get my head around the concepts.

"So yes, I am prepared for the breakdown of society I suppose, and no, I have nothing special to offer, I'm just doing my best in difficult circumstances."

"I'm hoping you're wrong," Kath blurted out, "but if you're right, then what about Fliss?"

My hand flew to my mouth. I had not even thought about Fliss, our lovely daughter away at university. How would she be getting on? There was no way I could contact her.

"So you haven't thought about her, as I suspected."

What was going on? Phil and Kath were normally so friendly. It was almost as if they held me responsible for what was happening. I felt hurt.

"Look, I'm trying to think things through but it's not easy. Please bear with me. Fliss will have to manage on her own for now; there are some things that won't wait."

"Exactly," said Greg. "Maslow's hierarchy."

"Pardon?" asked Kath.

"We had a lecturer at college who was keen on Maslow's Hierarchy of Human Needs, only he pronounced it Here-icky; I could never understand why. Basically, it points out that we all have fundamental needs like water, food, shelter etc, and these need to be attended to before you can go onto other needs like love and support or a satisfying job and all that sort of thing."

This was great. It was nice to have somebody else making the running for a change.

"So we need to sort out the most essential things and do them first. Matthew, your point about storing drinking water is absolutely right. The next task concerns fresh food. We don't want any of it going off if the power stays off. And that means going into town. I suggest the four of us go together."

"How are we going to pay?" I asked.

Phil was about to reply, then paused and gulped. Kath spoke first in a troubled voice.

"Don't tell me. If you're right Matthew, and it's a big if, then all the banking systems are not only down, they will remain down. The hole in the wall machines will not recognise our cards even when the power does come back on. In short, we're stuffed."

"The only money we can offer is the cash we have in our back pockets."

Greg was understating the problem, it seemed to me, but the time to debate all that was later.

"Let's take all the cash we have," I suggested. "My guess is that the shops will be reluctant to sell us anything because the tills will be down, but it's worth trying. I don't think looting will be an issue yet as we're still in the first few hours. I just need to leave a note for Mark. I know his exit looked dramatic, but he'll be fine. He'll come back when he's ready."

I was just looking for something to write with when there was a loud knock on the door. It was Georgina back again looking very concerned.

"Matthew, I was surprised that Reg wasn't at the meeting, so I've just been to check and there's no reply. I feel worried."

"Right, we'll call on the way to the shops," I announced. Reg was an elderly widower who had lived in the same house for sixty years, a few doors beyond Georgina up the road. A note for Mark would have to wait. It was his choice to react to the events of the morning in the way he had. Hopefully, he and I would be able to sort things out later. I quickly gave Timber a sweet to settle her, and we set off. After fifty yards, I regretted not leaving a note for Mark. That had been a mistake. It was hard to make good decisions with so much buzzing about in my head!

There was no reply from Reg when we knocked. I knew where the back door key was kept, under a drain cover round the back. I had often urged him to be more secure about his arrangements, but he insisted that he wanted people to be able to get in if there was an emergency.

We found him upstairs, lying on his bed, with an empty bottle of tablets beside him. He was faintly warm to the touch, but clearly dead. "Oh dear!" I said, somewhat lamely. Then a grim thought struck me; what had I said to him earlier that morning when I told him about the meeting? Enough to get him worried, clearly.

"Right. Well, he was nearer ninety than eighty. I daresay he has made a wise choice. However, it does bring to the fore something that has been troubling me. What are we going to do with the dead bodies?"

Kath was appalled. "Whatever do you mean?"

"Cremators are gas fired these days, and the likely number of deaths in coming weeks could make burials impractical it seems to me."

"Surely it hasn't come to that already! I can see you specialise in doom mongering," Greg said in a cheerful voice. I smiled. I was warming to him more and more. He picked up a blanket and briskly covered Reg up.

"Maslow," he declared. "Reg will have to wait. He'll be fine just where he is for now."

We went downstairs. Georgina stayed behind to empty the fridge while we set off up the road.

Chapter Five

There were plenty of people milling around the shopping centre looking lost. It turned out every shop was shut, and in most cases the owners were not in evidence. The covered shopping arcade was closed behind its heavy door, and standing in front was a lone policeman. Not for the first time when looking at a policeman I found myself thinking that he was just a boy. I must be getting old.

"It's no good hanging around here," said the constable as we approached. "You're better off at home."

"Can I introduce myself?" I said gently. I knew several of the local policemen, but not this one. "My name is Matthew Ridley Price and I am Neighbourhood Watch Co-ordinator for Standish Road, the end nearest the town centre. Do you need any help?"

"Thank you. I'm Bob. The Super will be here in a few minutes. If you could just stand back please."

I looked at Phil and Kath. They grasped my meaning and separated from Greg and me, making their way towards the multi storey car park where the ramp for the lorries bringing supplies to the shops lay. Ridley is my grandmother's maiden name, incidentally. I sometimes use it if I want to impress people.

"We'll wait over here," I called from the side. I could understand him not wanting to feel crowded. "Isn't it weird that cars, trains and planes all seem to be affected as well as the power."

He started. He clearly had not noticed the absence of planes.

"What do you make of it?" he called back.

This was not the moment to talk about power surges from the sun. "Whatever it is, it's not going to be sorted in a hurry. I'm concerned that the fresh food in the shops could be wasted if it is not given out soon. When your Superintendent comes, perhaps we can organise a distribution, one item per person. Form them up in an orderly queue, take their personal details, get a contribution out of them and issue the food. Anything to avoid looting. Same with the frozen food."

Bob hesitated. He was clearly going to prove an asset rather than a hindrance, it seemed to me. For one thing, he had turned up for work whereas most people had stayed at home. I reckoned his talk about his Super was simply designed to stall people. I decided to be more forthcoming.

"Look, suppose we tell everybody that in the present emergency, they each pay ten pounds as an entry fee and are allowed five items of fresh or frozen food only. Then we let in the first hundred, and every time someone comes out, one more is allowed in. I think the people would buy it. Do you have keys to get in?"

Phil and Kath returned while I was speaking. It was as we had hoped; nobody had tried to break in at the rear.

Bob did not hesitate. "Right, I was thinking along similar lines myself. I'd be glad of your help. We'll do it exactly as you say. OK, everybody."

His voice rang round the area, and everyone stopped to listen. We got them all to line up. Greg took the money, I counted them in, and Phil and Kath went in with Bob. Word soon got about, and the line was getting longer and longer. I tried to look as official as possible.

"Everybody needs to find all their screw cap bottles and fill them with drinking water when they get home. Turn the gas off at the main to prevent accidents."

I kept repeating the same advice over and over. And then, before I could prevent myself, I found myself adding "Open Air Hog Roast on Sunday at one o' clock in Standish Road, you're all welcome. Bring something to eat or drink to supplement."

Greg raised an eyebrow. "Oh yes?"

"We'll manage it somehow. The more this goes on the more I can see that if we are to get through, we all need to work together. It's no time for hanging back. A get-together will work wonders, you'll see."

It all worked like a charm. Some of the early people tried to take more than five items, but when they passed the queue, the shouts and noise were so threatening that they immediately handed their excess over and reduced their tally to five. Some people did not need to go into the shopping centre at all as a result. But even better, all the ones in the queue could see that if anybody tried to cheat, they would get short shrift, and it kept everybody in line. Bob was back outside by this time, and he was delighted by how things were going.

"Does the health food shop have a freezer?" I asked him. He thought it did, and hurried in to make sure that was accessible too. The lack of artificial light made it very gloomy inside, but people did not seem put out. A number of them thanked me for being so organised, and said they would definitely come on Sunday.

Within an hour, all the fresh food had been distributed, and the takings left in a carrier bag with Bob. I offered to accompany him to the police station but he declined.

The area was almost deserted by the time Bob locked up.

"We couldn't have managed it better," he chirruped. "Thanks for everything."

I shook his hand and we parted. He would definitely be there on Sunday he said.

On the way home I was able to push a note under the door of the butcher's, addressed to Charlie, whom I knew well, which read,

You are cordially invited to a Hog Roast in Standish Road on Sunday at 1300. In fact, you will be more than just welcome, because you are providing the hogs. Thanks in advance!
Matthew Price

When I got in, I remembered that Mark had stormed out of the back door and I had forgotten to lock it. Something made me go outside. I could see from where I was standing that the shed down the garden had been broken into.

This was serious. I went to have a look. The padlock was still in place, but the hasp had simply been unscrewed from the lintel. How absurd to have a good padlock but then only simple screws holding the ironwork in place. Daft! How had I overlooked that?

The only thing missing that I could see was my bike. This was a severe loss, it occurred to me. However, Sonia's bike was still there. I screwed the hasp back into place so that the shed looked secure, and took her bike indoors for safe keeping. It was likely to prove useful in the coming days.

The mystery was soon solved when Mark came riding onto the forecourt on my bike half an hour later, hammering on the door cheerfully. He was heavily laden and looked very pleased with himself.

"Look, Dad. I've bought you a present."

I wheeled the bike indoors. I didn't like to trust the shed again. Both bikes could go in my downstairs room for the time being.

The long brown cardboard box strapped on Mark's back proved to contain a brand new double-barrelled shotgun, and the two side panniers on my bike were loaded with boxes of cartridges. I was shocked.

"How did you..."

"Don't even ask," he interrupted, chuckling. "As soon as I heard what you were saying I thought we might be better off with these."

It turned out he had not been upset after all; he simply wanted an excuse to leave and riling me

31

seemed the best way of getting one. Great acting skills!

We had a simple salad from things in the fridge for supper. Only a few people showed up for the meeting, which did not last long; we agreed to meet at 1030 next morning. My coloured screw tops ran out quickly, but we arranged for someone to go to the collecting box at the church across town next morning and get more of them.

Mark did not want to be quizzed about the shotgun. I wondered at first whether he had stolen it. I did not want a vengeful farmer arriving here in the small hours, probably armed and determined. Then I remembered that he had tried his hand at clay pigeon shooting a year or two back. He had probably come by the shotgun through a contact from that time. This seemed somewhat reassuring.

Long after the evening's activities were concluded, and I had gone to bed, I was still lying awake turning things over. I managed to drift off to sleep eventually, but I had troubled dreams. There were dark days ahead, it seemed to me.

Chapter Six

I'm not going to give you a blow by blow account of our daily meetings; it would be too much, and I can't remember clearly enough anyway. However, a few incidents stand out in my mind.

One was a middle aged couple whom I did not know coming up to me before one of the meetings began. I think it might have been that second morning of what we came to call The Crisis. She was very tearful. The husband cleared his throat.

"Matthew, I'm Bruce and this is Sandra. Our daughter is backpacking in South East Asia on her gap year; she's due to go to university in September. From what you were saying yesterday, it seems we will not be able to contact her for a while. Do you have any thoughts?"

This was very difficult. I wondered what to say. I decided to be blunt.

"My own view is that you should not expect to hear from her for a long time, if at all." I winced as I said it, but it was no good pretending. They looked shocked. "I'm afraid she will have to manage as best she can in a foreign land. Travel will not be easy."

Then a thought struck me. "Is she alone?"

"Her boy-friend is with her."

"My hope is that they will grasp the seriousness of the situation, forget about trying to travel home for a while, and make a life together in a new continent."

The wife gave a sob, and Bruce looked very solemn. The impression I had was that I was confirming what they had already reckoned might be the case.

"Could they sail home, perhaps?"

A young man I did not know was joining in the conversation beside us. Before I could reply, Greg spoke from the other side.

"Difficult. Sailing boats will be at a premium, I reckon. People will need them to fish. There will be piracy. Personally, I would not like to land a boat on shore anywhere for fear of it being seized by force."

I was very unhappy about all this input. This couple were facing a major trauma, and half-thought out advice was not helpful!

"My guess is that your girl is level headed, thoughtful and responsible, judging from her two parents," I proposed. "Those characteristics will be invaluable, to my mind. Trust her to know what to do in her circumstances."

Bruce's mouth was set in a line. He clearly did not know what to say. Sandra burst into a fit of sobbing, and I found myself holding her in a hug. After a bit, I was able to detach myself and her husband took over. I felt awful speaking as I had done, but it would have been cruel to offer platitudes. The world had just got a whole lot larger, it seemed to me.

I caught Bruce's eye and detected a deep well of sadness. Neither of us could find any suitable words to say.

A second memory is of Greg explaining Maslow's principle to the group. We were all seated. Pamela had just said, "Shouldn't we go and see how they are getting on at the hospital?"

This was Starcross Community Hospital, not one of those huge rambling affairs with a bewildering array of wards, but small with plenty of day clinics for outpatients. However, there were some in-patient wards as well.

I motioned Greg to speak.

"Pamela, we simply don't have the resources to tackle every problem. We need to focus on the most basic needs of all, and get them right as a matter of priority. Water to drink comes top of the list, and it looks as if the water pressure, although weak, is holding up."

I suddenly had a mental image of a horse tethered to a beam walking round and round in a circle, led by an elderly man, working some hidden contraption in order to raise water from a well. I'm sure the device has some special name, but I don't know what it is. It's the kind of thing you used to see in old films occasionally. I hoped that the water works had their operation under better control than that. Not that I knew where the water works were.

Greg was continuing.

"Food comes next. It's no good relying on existing supplies as they will soon be exhausted. We need to brainstorm how we can get enough to eat."

This was too much for Pamela. "This is all very well, but I'm a trained nurse," she replied. "We can't just abandon the sick. I know where my duty lies."

"Fair enough", Greg said, "as long as we have enough hands on food production."

There was a lot more talk, but the immediate outcome was that Pamela took a few volunteers off with her to the hospital, while the rest of us sent a deputation to a local farmer who planted a crop of sweet corn each year. We reckoned it was about seedtime. Did he need any help? The fields and farm buildings were a mile or two out of town, beside a quiet road.

I find it hard to believe that anything is going to happen between Pamela and me. What with my suspicions as to why she is still single when she is so attractive, and her thinly veiled hostility towards me, it all seems rather unlikely. But then, maybe she treats all men like that? Perhaps she has some deep inner need to drive people off, but all the time she longs for intimacy, and if I were to persist she might prove to have a gentle melting heart? Like one of those dark chocolates which come in a box that I have a secret liking for. Anyway, is it still too early after Sonia to be thinking this way? I feel very uncertain.

When the deputation returned, the news was sombre. To save expense, farmers had got into the habit of hiring the machinery when it was required, rather than owning it outright, it seemed. This farmer, whose name was Bill, did have one small tractor which was working, but that was all. It was an old one, very basic, and ran on diesel. Unfortunately, his diesel storage tank was pretty low. However, when the group called at the local garage on their way back, they discovered that the manhole into which the tankers disgorged fuel had been forced. They had no way of being certain, but it looked as if the diesel and petrol had been taken.

However, at least the farmer had taken delivery of the seed. So it was that a day or two later, around three hundred of us set out on cycles on a sunny morning in a huge phalanx. The task was to create the holes for the seed to go in. Many of us had managed to find a suitable tool for the job to take with us.

Mark had been instrumental in drumming up people. "There will be entertainment," he assured us all. "Rudi and the Scarecrows. Music while you work." That sounded fun.

When we arrived, he opened a big rucksack which he had brought with him, and handed me my accordion which he had repaired in an amateur fashion (it had been in need of a new strap).

"You're the entertainment, Dad. I'm sorry about the Scarecrows – they were sadly unavailable at the last minute. I'm sure you'll cope." He laughed.

The cheeker! Accordion is not my *forte*, but it seemed that something was called for, so I started up with the theme tune to Captain Pugwash while the people were being allotted their rows for working, but on reflection that did not seem right for digging in the fields, so I tried Drunken Sailor next. That was worse; it required a minor chord, and although I am alright on the major ones, the minors have always eluded me. Also it was still on a seaside theme.

It was a relief when somebody started singing "One Man Went to Mow." I could manage that (only two chords). Before long, we were working our way through a whole lot of familiar favourites; Old

Macdonald had a Farm, Are you Going to Strawberry Fair and so on. Familiar to me, at any rate.

After a bit, I felt it was appropriate to stop. One can have too much of an accordion. I paused to admire the view across the fields to the distant hills. The sun was shining, and white clouds dotted the sky; a perfect Spring day. It was hard to believe that anything was wrong with the world, if you simply judged by appearances. I shook my head. It was weird.

The ground was not too hard, and digging the holes seemed not too difficult. After a few minutes, I eyed up the fields we had to cover and did a quick calculation. If we each dug three hundred holes, the job would be done. We might be finished by lunchtime

I miscalculated badly. The sun was going down by the time we completed the final hole and dropped the seed in, but we had done it. The sense of satisfaction was enormous.

The farmer was overwhelmed; he wept outright. He insisted that we accept something in payment. In the end, we went home with a splendid piebald horse called Broker. I found the name a little odd. Mark spotted a derelict cart surrounded by nettles in a corner of the farmyard and had the cheek to ask for it, and the horse was soon tethered to it. The suspension was almost non-existent, but Mark did not care a bit, cracking the reins with glee. The horse seemed to take to its new master, and set off at a fair trot.

We said our goodbyes and went over to our bikes. Just as we were getting ready to leave, we were astonished to see a heavy aeroplane fly overhead, very low, only about a hundred feet above the tree tops. It bore green and brown camouflage, had four propellers and made a deafening roar.

My instant feeling was one of deep dismay. It was so close, I could have shot it down with a quick right and left with my shotgun, I reckoned grimly.

Everybody stood stock still watching it flying Eastwards. Then when it disappeared from view there was a hubbub of conversation.

I kept my thoughts to myself. What was it? The words Troop Transporter came to mind, but it could have been carrying anything, or nothing. Why was it flying so low, dangerously low I thought? Was the army involved, or had it been stolen?

Questions, questions, always questions and no answers. This was the familiar pattern of those days. Personally I found the event very troubling and wondered what it might lead to.

On the way home, I called on Bruce and Sandra, the ones whose daughter was travelling. There was no reply, and to my horror, I could see them in their lounge sitting motionless. I called for help, which proved unnecessary as their back door turned out to be unlocked. They had taken tablets, like Reg had done, and were both dead. What a waste!

I was deeply shocked. Perhaps I had been wrong to be as blunt as I was, but at the time it seemed important to me not to create false hopes. I had not meant to dash all hope. But still, this seemed like an enormous over-reaction to me.

I had been going to ask them to find others who were in a similar plight to themselves and form a support group. Now it was too late. I felt a surge of anger; we could have benefited from their experience.

Then my eye fell on a framed photograph of a teenage girl on the coffee table. It must be their daughter. I felt a stab of sadness and pain. Her parents had taken my words as being final, but what if she and her boy friend managed to make it home again after all? What terrible news was going to greet them now?

We buried them at the old cemetery towards the crossroads, as we had done Reg. I felt most uncomfortable about the labour involved in the digging. People should be digging their own gardens instead, turning the lawns into vegetable plots, I reckoned. The words from the gospel "Leave the dead to bury their dead" sprang to mind.

I would need to raise the matter next week, but for now, it was time to focus on something much happier; Sunday's Hog Roast.

Chapter Seven

"Mark, will you please help me build the field oven?" I shouted from the foot of the stairs. It was Saturday morning. We have the bad habit in our family of calling each other from different rooms in the house when we are busy, rather than going to find them.

"Sorry, Dad, I'm too busy with The Overtakers, but I can help at lunchtime."

It was already ten in the morning; a two hour delay would not be a problem.

Mark had made Broker the horse and his ramshackle cart semi-presentable and was now offering a daily undertaking service along with his friends, only they called it The Overtakers. It was true that they were quicker than pedestrians, although it was easy to glide past their steady trot if you were on a cycle.

To my complete horror, Mark would ride up and down the local roads ringing a large hand bell he had found from somewhere, yelling "Any more dead bodies?" in a cheerful voice. I tried to silence him, but the little children said no; they loved it. Nothing Mark did could be wrong; they all looked up to him as their hero. He gave them rides in the cart and allowed them to stroke and fondle Broker, who seemed happy to receive the attention. I tried to warn the younger ones to keep away from the back legs of the horse, but of course they took no notice of me, and one received a kick for his pains. He was taken home howling, and after that the children were a little more careful of their huge pet.

Somebody produced a pre-digital camera which used film and so worked, and the children posed with their heads against Broker's flank, or in the case of some of the little ones against his knee; whether the photos would ever be developed and printed I rather doubted.

As nobody complained to me about my son's outlandish behaviour, I decided to retreat with honour by pretending I did not belong, which suited everybody fine.

People used to come out of their houses at the sound of the bell and ask Mark if he could look out for this or that, and in due course, he and his friends built quite a thriving business. I was pleased; it was good that my boy should be flourishing as a rag and bone man. Indeed, he was in his element. All his gloom had evaporated.

Towards lunchtime he turned up to help, as good as his word. There had been no deaths last night, he explained.

"Now," I announced, "I have always wanted to make an army field kitchen since my father told me about it when I was a teenager, and at last I have the chance. It works like this. You bury a barrel in the ground, about half submerged in the earth. The base of the barrel should have a hole in it, and an underground chimney should be created to allow the smoke to escape. We could use a drainpipe. So an uphill site is required ideally, with the open end of the barrel pointing downhill."

I sketched a quick pencil drawing on the back of an old envelope to explain. (Might a local postal service become a possibility in time, I wondered in passing?).

"Then you mound up earth and turfs over the barrel like this," (more pencil strokes), "beat it down hard, fill the barrel with firewood and combustibles, and ignite. You need a really good blaze. The barrel itself burns, the surrounding earth is baked hard and absorbs the heat, and hey presto, you have a piping hot oven when you have raked out the dying embers. What do you reckon?"

"No prob Dad. I'll get the boys onto it."

We chose the grass verge at the beginning of the triangle at the head of the road as our site. The barrel had come from a local garden centre. It was actually two half barrels, designed for growing fruit trees, but they worked well enough.

It proved to be a good deal harder to make than it sounds, and more than once I wondered whether we would succeed, but in the end we had a good setup. I felt encouraged.

At one stage during the afternoon, there was a gradually increasing roar and a car shot past us, heading for the town. This was totally unexpected; we had not seen a car all week. We all stared.

"Old banger, pre 1990," I declared. No micro processor on board to be fried.

The impression I had from its sound was that it had received little servicing since it rolled off the forecourt twenty years earlier. A minute or two later, it was shooting back towards us, having simply driven round the triangle at high speed. I waved for it to stop, hoping for news of the outside world, but the driver made an aggressive gesture and roared past.

"*Imbecilo!*" I yelled, for the sake of the Italian neighbours, and then at the top of my voice, "You Expletive Deleted Expletive Deleted!" There was no danger that he might hear and come back, driving at that speed.

I turned to see Mark's friends looking oddly at me. They clearly thought this behaviour was out of character.

"Boy racer. It's good to let off a little steam occasionally," I smiled. I could see they were quite amused.

Sunday dawned fine, and we lit at seven. There was quite a little crowd out to watch, even at that early hour. We were already learning to rise with the sun and go to bed early to save candles. I wondered how many would turn up at lunchtime.

Charlie the butcher had come up trumps as I was sure he would. He had plenty of pork in whole pigs, and as I suspected, he had no means of keeping his walk-in fridge cold, so they all needed to be eaten. Some of them he was able to salt down, until the salt ran out. How daft was that, I reflected? Of all the substances in the world, salt is probably the one that will last the longest. But it was one thing to say that and another to get it from Nantwich in Cheshire or wherever the nearest salt mine was.

I arranged for Bob the policeman to give Charlie some of the takings from the shopping centre as payment.

Incidentally, we had established a pattern that first day at the supermarket without realising it. The shopping arcade was opened up each morning, by a team Bob the policeman had gathered around him, and people paid to be allowed in, ten pounds until the food ran out, and then just five pounds thereafter. They were allowed one bagful of items each. Naturally the tins and jars went first; long dated food items were the new gold, it seemed to me. The principle was, no hoarding. I had explained carefully to our meeting that anybody who hoarded ran the risk of being attacked, and it was better to live simply. People got the point. Many of our folk showed plenty of character in those early days.

The oven worked like a charm. The meat went in at 1130, and at one o' clock it was done to a turn.

People had been arriving since ten, as it was a fine day and there was nothing else to do, and it was a great place to find out what was happening. We must have had a couple of thousand that first Sunday; in future weeks numbers would swell to five thousand or more.

Despite the hardships of the week we had just had, everybody was in a good mood. The children were thrilled at the unexpected holiday, which was how they interpreted the lack of school. Mark had found a 1930s wind-up gramophone with a horn for a speaker and a stack of seventy-eight records in Reg's loft, and the young people were having a great time jiving to Jazz. After a bit, the clockwork would reach a point of exhaustion and begin to run down, which was the signal to the dancers to go into slow motion and eventually freeze, to great merriment.

I couldn't help wondering if this running-down was a preview of what was to come over the coming months, but I pushed the thought out of my mind. Worrying was for later; this was a day to enjoy ourselves.

People had bought their own plates and mugs and fold up chairs, very sensibly, and there was a good deal of alcohol to be had. Conversation flowed freely.

I spotted Pamela with a man on her arm; she avoided meeting my eye. I felt a pang of envy. Why had I been so slow?

A number of people I knew from around the town came up to say hello. Among them was Valerie, with her husband and the two children.

"Here is your money," she insisted, passing me her wages for the cleaning which never took place.

The children ran off while we adults found chairs, and sat down.

"Well," I explained to them, "it seems to me that this money you are holding is not worth what it was a week ago."

They looked at me.

"In one sense, it's worth more than it was. The collapse of computers means the collapse of banks and even of whole currencies, if you think about it. It's a long time since all money was represented by cash, after all. You might be able to persuade someone to accept an IOU by showing them a recent bank statement, I suppose, but I doubt it, as there is no guarantee that any bank or building society will ever give you any cash again. I reckon all electronic cash, as it were, is gone for good."

They weren't happy about this; like most people, they still believed that what we were experiencing was only temporary.

"Anyway," I persevered, "all people actually have as we speak is the money in their wallets. So you could argue instead that cash is worth more than it was, it seems to me. In that instance, you should be offering me back less. Take your pick."

"But surely," her husband said, "things will get back to normal before too long?"

"They might do," I replied. It was a mistake to be too hard on them; they had not been at our meetings. "But answer me this. Where are all the people that should be stepping into the breach? Where is the Mayor, and the councillors, and people like that?"

We agreed they were notable by their absence. I was just going to say that I bet the wealthier people with their second home in the country had done a bunk which would delay any return to normality when one of Mark's friends came racing up on his cycle.

"I think you had better come," he gasped. "It's looking bad."

I made my excuses, hurried off for my own bike, and was soon pedalling behind the boy towards the church at the other end of the road.

Mark and his friends were arguing with a group of about twenty other young people outside the church door. It looked ugly to me. I went up.

"What seems to be the trouble?" I inquired.

"Where's God and the church when you need them!" said a lad angrily. "They're a bunch of hypocrites."

I did have some sympathy with him, having wondered myself why the local clergy had not been out doing more. They seemed to think their job was to maintain the worship of their flock, what they called the 'services'. I couldn't get it myself. I used to be a churchgoer in my younger days, and the sermon which had impressed me most had been about the two words 'worship' and 'service'. Although these are separate words in English, it seemed that in both the Hebrew of the Old Testament and the Greek of the New Testament the two concepts were rendered by just one word. So that meant that you needed both, the preacher had said; worship without serving your fellow human beings is an insult to God, and service without worship was also no good, although I forget what reason he gave for that. I just cottoned on to the first part of his message. All my adult life, I reckoned, the church had become more and more worship-orientated to the exclusion of acts of love and compassion to people in need, losing its biblical roots in the process, to the point where I had lost enthusiasm for going any more.

But this was no time for a theological debate. They had stones in their hands and were starting to throw them towards the church windows.

"Please," I urged, "don't cause any damage because it will be hard to get anything repaired. By all means shout but don't throw stones! PLEASE!"

They did take some notice of me. One boy yelled, "God you bastard!" to general laughter. Then, with all the predictability of a shoal of fish in the sea, they had all had enough and swirled off in a different direction.

"Thanks Dad," Mark called, going with them. I was left looking at the damage, which was not too extensive. The windows were made of leaded lights, and most were protected by wire netting, but some had been broken.

After a few moments, a frightened lady poked her head out of the church hall, which stood slightly behind the church.

"It's alright, they've gone," I called.

She produced a huge old key, and together we made our way into the building. There was a scattering of broken glass and stones in the aisle. As we were clearing them up, some words from the Gospel floated into my mind: 'My house shall be a house of prayer for all nations, but you have made it a den of thieves!'

I found this rather disconcerting. In what sense was this church today a den of thieves? Who was being robbed of what?

I found I couldn't make sense of it and gave it up. The lady was full of gratitude. She looked as if she recognised me but couldn't think from where.

"My wife used to come here sometimes," I explained.

As we were leaving, I looked round. The old pews had been replaced by moveable chairs, which could be stacked if necessary, creating a large space. The building might be needed before we were through. Then I had a thought; why were churches so unnecessarily high? One could put in at least one mezzanine floor, probably two. Was there a scaffolding firm in our town that could put up something temporary? It would create a lot of extra accommodation. An idea to store away for next Winter. Why, the combined body heat of all those people would help raise the temperature a bit, even if it was rather noisy. A latter day Noah's Ark, I found myself reflecting, where really, if you think of it, the noise of all those animals cooped up in a small space must have been deafening.

The numbers were definitely fewer at the hog roast when I got back, probably because all the food and drink had gone. As the last people made their way, they were keen to say that they would be back next week.

I felt pleased. The day had been a success. It was so important that we pull together, and so far, that was the predominant mood. The trick was to get it to last.

Chapter Eight

One excellent outcome of the hog roast was that everybody was more ready to believe that we were in for the long haul. It was the absence of authority figures, the 'they' that we have all learned to rely on to keep things running, that did it. It had become clear that we were on our own.

It was only day six, and we were getting into our stride. One could hardly ask for more.

Incidentally, I think the day sowing sweet corn might have been after the hog roast rather than before; it is difficult to be clear about the order of events. Not that it matters much, but I like to be precise where possible.

A major development in week two was the soup kitchen. It was Mark who spotted that there was a solid fuel stove in Reg's house, not in the kitchen, but out the back. It had clearly not been used for years, as it was piled high with rubbish – old cardboard boxes full of newspapers going back decades, hundreds of rotting supermarket plastic bags, muddy Wellington boots and so forth. We got it all cleared out and inspected the stove. To my delight, it was an old-fashioned cast iron one. The chimney appeared to be sound; it should all function, we reckoned.

We fetched kindling and logs from our garden, placed them inside on a bed of screwed up newspaper, struck a match (a wonderful invention I have often thought) and closed the door. It was obvious which vent should be left open to supply an up draught. Within a few minutes, we had a good blaze and the stove began to grow warm to the touch.

"Excellent," I declared. "Well done, Mark. This is going to be good."

Now the question was, who to ask to head things up? Instantly I knew the answer; Georgina. We walked the hundred yards to her door. She was in and answered when we knocked.

"Georgina, I've got a job for you. Will you run a soup kitchen for the community, please?"

She was a bit taken aback.

"The thing is," I continued, "all of us are having difficulty creating hot food due to the gas and electricity being down. Mark and I have just discovered a solid fuel stove at Reg's house, and it's in full working order. There's a good blaze up already. It ought to be possible to find plenty of fuel for it. My idea is that we run his ground floor as a soup kitchen for all of us, quite literally. What we need is a team cutting up vegetables and whatever ingredients there are to hand, and a chef boiling them up on the hob. Then the people can call in for hot soup. What do you think?"

"Great idea. And it sounds like fun. I'd love to do it."

So it was settled. Before long, word had got about. Georgina was not short of volunteers for the cutting up and cooking, and The Overtakers took on the job of collecting suitable ingredients on their rounds. They also spread the word; people were to bring their own mugs to save washing up, and the

Soup Scullery as it came to be called would be open from 1000 until 1800 each day.

At first there were just a few who took advantage of the new service, but within a fortnight, numbers had swelled so much that it was continuous serving from dawn till dusk. There was a one way system, enter by the front door and leave by the back door. People would bring gifts of fuel as well; not just logs but broken furniture and even paperback books. I was horrified to see a Bible being confined to the flames on one occasion, but said nothing.

Naturally, the Soup Scullery became a centre for news and views, but after a day or two, hand-written notices began to appear on the fence posts in the garden, offering skills.

Roof Repairs, 30 Lambourne Drive

Grow Your Own Veg
Training and Equipment
Number 6 The Pines

and so forth. We soon had a proper notice board erected, which turned into a whole series of notice boards after a bit; one for Trades, another for Wanted, and rather touchingly after a few days, one for Thanks.

I used to cast my eye up and down the announcements fairly regularly. There was an unsigned one:

Thanks for the ten pounds somebody pushed
through our letter box,
you've no idea how much it meant to us. (Family
of six)

Once again I wondered how much cash was going to matter in this new world we had been propelled into.

Then my eye fell on a strange trade.

Teeth Care – Holistic, Natural and Olde Worlde.
Honest Tradesmen's Pliers used for teeth
removal.
Free scale and polish with Genuine Woodcarver's
Chisel.
Close shave with the Originalle Cut-Throat Razor.

It was all written in pencil, in a schoolboy hand. Then my eye travelled on down to the foot of the page, and I saw my own name and address there.

"MARK!" I yelled, but he was nowhere near. That boy!

Incidentally, was original ever actually spelt that way?

I made to remove it, but then on reflection, I left it where it was. It did seem humorous, and we all needed something to smile about. Truth to tell, I was rather pleased by it really. Mark was doing very well, I reckoned.

Nobody ever called on me for assistance, but they might have done; all the town's dentists remained closed. Couldn't one of them have offered a limited service, without drilling, naturally?

The Soup Scullery turned out to be the solution to something that had been both a delight and a concern to me. At the first Hog Roast, I had announced a competition to the children; who could hand in the most screw-top bottles and jars? "They must have a tight-fitting lid", I explained, "and each one will earn you a penny."

The financial reward occurred to me after the discussion about the value of money that afternoon. I was interested to see what the children's attitude to coins would be, and as we had an accumulation of pennies and two-penny pieces in tins at home, into which I used to empty my coppers to save unnecessary wear on my trouser pockets, it seemed like a good solution all round.

The children's interest was kindled. Our home was soon filling up with screw top bottles and jars, to Mark's consternation. It was hard to get him to see how valuable these were going to be in due course.

Now that the Soup Scullery was proving popular, it became obvious that no family could live in the rest of the house, with all those people tramping through, so the upstairs was given up to bottle storage. I had never seen so many jars; the rooms were filling up.

Then one afternoon I received a call from an irate mother, accompanied by a red-faced youth of about nine. He had torn his clothes trying to climb in to the local dump, looking for more bottles for my 'wretched scheme', it transpired.

Although outwardly apologetic, I was inwardly thrilled. One of the children had remembered not only that there might be unbroken bottles in the bottle bank, but that there was also a tops bank there too. Brilliant!

Within fifteen minutes I was at the dump with my sledgehammer and some wedges, along with some of the teenagers. It was great that they had seized on the bottles idea so warmly. They seemed more open to new ideas than many of the adults.

The gates were tall and forbidding and firmly locked. I managed to slide a wedge into an appropriate place near the lock, and then let rip with a few well-aimed blows; the gates shivered and then obligingly separated. The boys pushed them back and secured them open. There would be no need to lock people out of the dump for the time being, as our aim was not to leave unwanted rubbish at unwelcome hours, but rather to remove items once thought waste but now seen as precious. There would be wood to burn, and other useful things as well. I smiled inwardly; it was a considerable transformation of attitude in only a few short weeks.

It was next morning that there was a knock on our door. As I made my way to open it, I became aware of a small crowd of young people outside. There were hoarse whispers of "No, Stacey!" and "Let Stacey, come on Stacey."

I was curious. I opened wide to discover twelve or fifteen children. The older ones were shepherding the younger ones. In the middle was a girl aged only about five or six, clutching a plastic bag full of bottles and jars which she could only just lift. Her face was red, and there was a curl of hair inclined to fall into one eye. She moved forward shyly, to give me the bag.

"You must be Stacey," I said in a friendly voice as I took it graciously. The girl looked mightily relieved, and nodded vigorously.

"She has collected one hundred and thirty-eight bottles," an older girl said, probably her sister. The rest of them were all carrying bags of jars and bottles as well I observed.

"Wonderful!" I exclaimed. "They will be such a help for bottling fruit in the weeks to come."

As we all carried the spoils of war as I thought of them up to Reg's house, I talked to another of the older ones. They had worked as a group, she explained, but most of it was Stacey's idea. They had investigated the local bottle banks as well as people's bins.

"Before The Crisis, I used to push my bottles into the bottle bank hard, so to speak, thinking that if they all broke, the bank would hold more before it needed emptying," I explained by way of conversation as we walked along. "I thought I was doing somebody a favour!"

The girl nodded. She was clearly not fully at her ease talking to a strange adult. I thought I would try some humour to ease things along.

"Do you know this song?" I enquired, and launched into the well-known song Waltzing Matilda, but with different words.

Recycling Matilda, recycling Matilda,
Who'll come recycling Matilda with me?
And he laughed as he thrust her forearm down the bottle bank,
Who'll come recycling Matilda with me!

"It is a bit gruesome," I added, but the girl thought it was funny. I would not have sung it had there been any adults present, naturally. People can be so sticky about things like that.

We added the jars and bottles to the piles in the bedrooms. Some of the children had a quick soup from the Scullery downstairs to keep them going.

"Everything under control?" I called to the volunteers in their aprons cutting up vegetables in the kitchen.

"Yes," they all responded.

"You see? The age of miracles is not over!" I replied. They laughed.

The children ran off happily, but not before I had thanked Stacey very much once again. She was thoroughly pleased as she went off skipping along; it had made her day.

There were happy times in those early days; it was only those of us who thought about events that had a general sense of oppression. The thing to do was to capitalise on the good and hope it would last.

Chapter Nine

While I was with the children, I noticed what I had observed before, that the people queuing for soup would only have a cursory look at the notice boards while they were passing. I felt concerned about this. It was a matter of life and death, quite literally, that we all pull together. I decided therefore to alter my strategy somewhat. I tried to commit an hour or two each day to simply standing where people approached the front door of the house and talking to them. Naturally I listened to whatever they had to say, and learnt a great deal from it, but I also had a policy known only to myself of speaking to some people about the need to conserve water, and to others about growing vegetables 'in case The Crisis goes on for a while'. I hoped to get the message out widely.

The result was not what I had expected. Because of a complete vacuum of leadership from our community leaders, who seemed to have evaporated quite frankly, people started calling me the Mayor when they thought I was not listening.

At first I felt rather embarrassed about this, but before long I decided that if that was how they wanted to react, then well and good; there were more important things at stake than worrying about personal status.

Incidentally, I did have an insight into the process of evaporation for want of a better term.

As a somewhat older person, what one might call a man of mature middle age, I sometimes need to get up in the middle of the night to go to the loo. Now that we were trying to save water, the obvious thing was for me to use a chamber pot and empty it at the far end of the garden each day to save flushing the toilet.

You may think I was perhaps over-conscientious, but it seemed to me that it would be possible to save the water needed to cleanse the chamber pot if I went in the garden direct, as it were. The nights were mild with the approach of summer, so feeling cold on going outside was not an issue.

On getting up, I would pause to give Timber the briefest stroke as I passed her on the landing, she raising her head fractionally to indicate that this was called for, tiptoe down to the hall, slip on my sandals, unlock the back door and go into the back garden. It is not overlooked by other houses.

At first I used to wee at the far end of the garden, but more recently I have been conducting an experiment with the vegetable plot. I think, but I may be wrong, that urine should help the veg. I don't let anything fall on the plants, you understand, although given the amount of rain in our country it probably would not matter if I did, but rather I go near the roots. Sort of beside them. I have chosen a few plants for the experiment, which is effectively like a daily dose of medication for them, I suppose, and deliberately neglected others. It would have been better if it could have been a double blind trial, really, if you know about that sort of thing, but I can't see how to arrange that. But at least I can ask others to say how they think the veg are doing rather than simply relying on my own opinion, which helps make the experiment a little more objective.

It would have been nice to look the subject up in an encyclopaedia, but ours have gone out long ago being replaced by the internet, and a trip to the town library would be fraught with difficulties, although Bob the policeman could probably let me in if I asked him. So I'm undertaking original research, following the scientific method. Heigh-ho for Isaac Newton!

Sorry, I seem to be feeling somewhat skittish today.

There's another reason why I enjoy my nightly trips outside, and that is to observe the wild life. More than once I have spotted a fox slinking away in the shadows, and if you listen closely there is almost always some little creature around. I wish I knew their names, but the truth is that I would not recognise a vole or shrew if it was close up in daylight.

After a week of this, I finally realised what was going on in my thinking. Since The Crisis broke, I have grasped that not only do we all need each other, we need the animal world as well. People talk about vermin, but I am coming to see foxes, for instance, more as our friends.

I need to digress in order to explain what I mean.

One of my roles recently has been going round the neighbourhood with my long-handled water key turning off the water stopcock in vacant properties, and my triangular-shaped small key which opens the gas meter boxes to turn off the gas. If I discover a house that appears empty, I contact the neighbours first.

"Oh yes," one said recently for example, "Mustapha has taken his family away to the Middle East."

If the neighbours don't themselves have a key, they usually know somebody who has got one, and then we go in together. I don't like to go alone, for fear of being accused of misconduct in some way. I empty the fridge and freezer and pedal bin (the neighbours have never thought of all three of these) and divide the contents into three piles. What is still edible goes to the neighbours. What is fit for animals goes to Broker and Timber and one or two of her local friends, which just leaves the food that is going off.

My policy on this is to spread it on the ground as far from the house as I can, generally at the far end of the garden. You ask why? Well, there is not going to be a rubbish collection again soon, so really we are reliant on so-called vermin to consume what would otherwise go badly rotten and become a health risk if left in a bin. I think it is the best way.

In short, every society needs its vultures and should value them, although I would not myself like to keep a vulture as a pet.

You may be wondering why I have a long-handled key for turning off the water main stopcock.

A few years ago, when Timber was out with me in the garden doing her last things before bed-time (why is this chapter so full of weeing in the garden?) I heard the sound of water pouring down onto concrete from three doors up the road, Georgina's house in fact. It did not sound right at all, so when I had taken Timber in, I explained the situation to Sonia, and walked along the road to see what was happening.

Sure enough, a cascade of water was pouring out from an overflow pipe just below the roof onto the concrete outside Georgina's back door.

I rang her doorbell, but there was no reply, so I called on Dwight, an American businessman who rents the house next door further on up the road. He confirmed she was away and he had a key, so we made our way into her kitchen and searched hard for the stopcock, which we failed to find. So then we located the main stopcock out in the road. This was about a metre below the ground down a long tube, and try as I might, I could not turn it, even lying on my front and ruining my shirt in the process. I suppose it was very stiff from not having been turned in a long time. Stopcocks can get like that.

So all we could do was to ring the Water Board. It was gone midnight by this time, and they said they would send someone out to turn off the water in the road. Dwight and I retired to our houses for well-earned sleep leaving the water pouring out. Before we left, I placed a piece of timber I found under the cascade at an angle, to ensure that the worst of the downpour was deflected away from the house lest Georgina end up with a damp problem.

Imagine my feelings when at nine o' clock next morning the water was still pouring out. Such a waste! Why couldn't the water people have been true to their word?

However, Dwight had his head screwed on and acted shrewdly. We went back in to the house and searched by the phone in the hall for Georgina's address book which we soon found. He made a few calls to family members and quickly located her staying with her brother not far away. She arranged to come home immediately, and by midday the waterfall ceased.

The end of the story is that the problem was caused by rust on the ball-cock in the header tank. All it took was one tiny hole the size of a pin-prick for the ball to fill with water and then to plunge down in the tank, allowing the cold water from the main to flood in. It would happen while she was away!

I suppose it's a picture of what has happened to our society in a way. One tiny slip and look at the mess we're in.

Back to the animals. It is not just the foxes and birds that have their place helping us out, but also farmyard animals. Our day sowing the sweetcorn seed was not just a one off. Most people had enjoyed the day, and over the next few weeks we visited other farms in the area with offers of help. So it was that we came to have a couple of goats, which were useful in keeping lawns under control, being passed along the road from house to house; a cow, and any number of chickens.

My parents used to keep chickens after the war for a few years. I must have been three or four at the time. I remember them building the hen house and hen coop as we called them. I made sand castles with the liquid concrete when they weren't looking; it was fascinating stuff and coloured my clothes grey.

I have a happy memory of seeing a score of baby chicks cheeping away in a small enclosure on our kitchen floor of all places, with a bright lamp suspended above them for warmth.

Now we had four young chickens of our own. They lived in the car. This proved ideal. At night, the windows were left open an inch which allowed the air to circulate but kept the foxes out, and by day the chickens were allowed to roam about on the forecourt.

One of them turned out to be a cockerel. He liked to stand on the steering wheel and start the day for us all at some unearthly hour with an apoplectic fit of crowing.

For bedding, we found that torn-up newspaper was good. The children loved collecting the eggs, and some learned how to milk the cow and goats. All in all, I reflected, our road was slowly coming to look like an urban farm. Perhaps we might pull through, I found myself wondering. Dare I begin to hope?

I tried to befriend the chickens. One afternoon, I took one of our garden chairs on to the forecourt and sat in it for an hour, hoping they might come close enough for me to touch one. No such luck; they were too interested in looking for any stray morsels of corn from their breakfast which might have lodged between the crazy paving stones.

However, they took a shine to Broker, I noticed. Normally he was kept on a school playing field nearby ("Plenty of grass, Dad," as Mark explained), but occasionally he would be tethered to the fence on out forecourt (I couldn't find a respectable metal ring in my shed). Then the chickens would sidle up to him, making that funny noise hens make, while he would just stand there, swishing his tail occasionally to keep the flies off.

I felt a little unhappy about this. What has that horse got that I haven't got?

Oh yes, I nearly forgot. Back to me fertilising the vegetable plants.

One night when I was out there admiring the stars, which looked better than ever with all the street lights off, it being a clear night even though there was a half moon near the horizon, I became aware of a car gliding almost silently past out in the road. Its engine was running, but from the sound I reckoned the vehicle was in neutral.

Instantly I raced along the passage beside our house, seized the wooden gate and lifted it as much as I could to stop it from grating, opened it and ran out into the road. I was just in time to see the tail lights of a truck with an open back fading into the distance, moving away from the town.

So that was how the great and the good were leaving. They presumably had a country cottage or something similar, and an older vehicle which was not compromised by the failure of the silicon chips. The thing to do was to keep their departure secret, and then do a moonlight flit one night while the rest of us were sleeping.

I could not honestly blame them. Mark had raised the idea of us doing something similar in the early days, but I had said no, once a Neighbourhood Watch Co-ordinator always a Neighbourhood Watch Co-ordinator. I was going to carry out my duties as best I could. He could see I was in earnest and accepted it. We were here for the duration.

Anyway, I said, what guarantee was there that the roads would be clear? There might be highwaymen operating out there by now for all we knew. Law and order had gone, if you stopped to think about it, as there was no-one to enforce the law, and it was only a tradition of being law-abiding citizens that was holding us together, and we needed to nurture that.

As the tail lights dimmed and faded, I felt a deep sense of sadness. A truck like that could have been such a help to us here. What a tragedy it was that the reaction of everybody seemed to be to look after number one first and foremost. If only everyone had stayed at their posts, things might have gone very differently. But they had not, and that was that.

Perhaps it was less than noble of me, but before coming back indoors, my eyes strayed over to Pamela's house, or rather, to her bedroom, which I presumed was one of the upstairs windows, unless of course she slept out the back. All was dark, as I had expected. Had she been unable to sleep, there might have been the light of a flickering candle, but there wasn't.

"God bless – sleep well!" I mouthed without sound in her direction. I feel very lonely at times.

Chapter Ten

I knew we were beaten when the refugees from London started arriving in earnest. At first it was only a trickle. They brought grim stories with them of looting and violence. There had apparently been a huge fire somewhere which had affected an industrial estate and part of a residential road; no fire engines had come, so it lasted several days, and it had only been put out by the torrential rain.

This intrigued me, because we had had no rain here to speak of. On the contrary, I was beginning to be concerned about the vegetables not getting enough water. Strange.

Greg took on the task of settling the new arrivals in. Some needed medical attention, which fell to Pamela and her team. Her man turned out to be a medic, which I might have guessed really. I had been completely wrong to oppose her over the hospital as I had. She had lost all interest in me, if she ever had any.

One of the major issues early on – I ought to have told you before, really – was whether we were going to put a barrier across the road at the end pointing towards London, away from the town centre. Ours was not the main road, but all the same, that would be the direction from which trouble would come, if it was going to. The debate took place in one of our daily meetings. Incidentally, they only lasted a week, as numbers soon began dropping. Everyone was busy with their own concerns, it seemed.

I felt very strongly about this matter, but I resisted the urge to express my view. It seemed wiser to let others do the speaking.

All the attitudes that one might have expected were voiced, for and against. In the end, to my huge relief, the vote was for no barrier. As somebody pointed out, I think it was Phil, how were we going to defend any such barrier if we made one? We had no weapons. (I kept quiet about my shotgun). People would be better shoring up their own houses if they wanted to. The road was a corridor, an open public space, and so forth.

To my mind, it was all an extension of the hoarding argument. A barrier would have been an attempt to hoard our living space, as it were. And also, what about the plane we had seen? I still did not know what to make of that, but it spoke of armed strength greater than we could muster.

Personally, I wanted to put up a board at the London end of the road saying

Welcome to Starcross.
Your Contribution is Much Appreciated

or something similar, but this was ruled out. Shame, really.

Anyway, Greg did a grand job. A huge sign saying Accommodation Office appeared outside his house. When people arrived, we directed them there. They were made to sign various ledgers to the effect that the houses they occupied were only on loan, and then given the keys.

I was in demand with my long handled water key, and I soon found myself going back round the houses I had visited earlier as I explained to you, turning the water back on, urging people not to use the loo, etc. We also encouraged residents to make sure that all the electrical appliances in our houses were unplugged, so that if by any miracle the power did come back on, it would not be defeated by a sudden huge demand.

I noted that the children had done a good job with the litter pick. They seemed to have taken to me, not only as Mark's Dad, but also because of the bottles and jars, which kept on coming, by the way. I asked them to keep the area litter free, and gave them my long-handled litter picking tongs (it must have a snappy name, surely). You work the little lever at the top, and a pair of jaws opens and shuts at the bottom. With practice, you get quite proficient at it, although chewing gum stuck to the pavement tends to defeat it.

The youngsters enjoyed using it, and earned praise from me in the process. It is fun to have a go at it.

In a month or so, it would be time to get the children on fruit pick. This was not a year to allow rotten apples to fall to the ground uncared for!

We kept the weekly hog roasts going, somehow. We had not had to adopt Mark's suggestion so far, thankfully.

"It's a natural development, Dad," he explained, "and only requires a side-slip of three letters; we move on to Dog Roast."

I suppose I should have laughed, as it was meant to be funny, but in fact I felt an instant shiver of concern for Timber.

What I actually said was, "Mark it's four letters, or even five depending on how you count them."

"Dad, you're so serious!" Mark came back. "Lighten up!"

They keep on saying this to me in our family, but I don't think it's fair. I have tried to keep humour in my life and crack the odd joke. How much more do they want from me? I am trying. Honest!

When all the houses were occupied, we instituted the one person per room rule. This meant that you could not say your house was full until your residents equalled your rooms, excluding toilets kitchens and bathrooms. Once again, the principle was to avoid hoarding living space. One day the quota would need to go up to one and a half, and then later to two.

On one occasion I searched out the vicar of the church and sounded him out about allowing people to live in the church building. His response was one of outrage.

"This is God's house; it's out of the question to allow squatters to live in it!"

I wanted to reply, "This is God's house; it's out of the question to keep homeless people out," but I refrained. I could see there was no progress to be made in that quarter. It was a shame, because I had come up with a part solution to the noise problem if we had put the mezzanine floors in.

The thump of people above walking on the planks resting on scaffolding poles would have been highly disturbing to people below, especially if teenagers chose to jump up and down to heighten the effect. However, there was a carpet superstore two or three hundred yards away, and I reckoned that with enough people, we could have staggered along to the church carrying a roll of carpet such as those places have, heaved it up the ladders and laid it over the planks. Those rolls have a width of four metres approximately, so three or four of them laid out side by side would have been sufficient to have done a whole floor.

However, as there was no scaffolding firm in Starcross, and no permission was forthcoming from the Vicar, there was nothing I could do. Never mind.

With the never-ending influx, it would have easy to give way to depression. Instead, I made a decision that whatever happened, I was going to keep on doing my duty as best I could and not flinch, no matter how much my heart was telling me that it was hopeless. It required some guts, I can tell you. Some days I simply wanted to lie down and die before I forgot what the good times before The Crisis had been like. Looking back on it from our new perspective, it struck me that life back then had been incredibly cushy, and that few of us had appreciated that fact.

Oh yes, one thing that the refugees initiated without realising it was to do with the swimming pool.

The family moving into Mustapha's house were thrilled to see there was a swimming pool in the garden, until they realised it was empty. It seemed odd that there should be one in our road, as we were not a well-heeled district, so I made some enquiries. It turned out that previous owners of the house had had a daughter who was an actress in a TV soap opera and made a lot of money, so that led to the swimming pool.

"Put the plug in it, and gather all the rain water you can," I suggested. "You might have a paddling pool by the summer."

We found a tarpaulin and some rope, and with a little ingenuity, we were able to rig it up with one end up in some fruit trees and the other over the pool so that when it rained, water would run off it into the pool.

Then it hit me between the eyes; why wasn't every house doing that? We all had these large areas of roof channelling the rain into gutters and then into down pipes, which ran into soakaways beneath the garden. All we had to do was to install a water butt or equivalent at the foot of the down pipe and hey presto we had extra water whenever it rained; not high quality or drinkable, admittedly, but useful none the less.

We even had a water butt in the passage outside our house that led to the side gate. It was standing upside down to keep the water out, would you believe!

Let me explain. We bought it twenty-five years ago to catch rainwater from the roof for the garden in dry weather, but it had tended to fill with rotting leaves and became unpleasantly smelly, so we removed it and I put it out of sight behind the shed down the garden. I did not reflect on the matter at the time; it was simply a case of eliminating the smell. But now I realised that since our neighbours had chosen to take out their Wisteria, which had climbed all over our house as well as theirs and got too big, the leaf problem had been sorted, and the water from the roof should be cleaner. Also, it ought to be possible to make a sieve arrangement to catch any leaves with a little ingenuity.

It took me all of three minutes to unscrew the extra length of down pipe that I had installed when taking the butt out and slot the beastie back in. The plinth on which the butt stood was still in place, allowing one to fill a watering can from the little black tap near the bottom of the butt.

Perhaps I will just explain why the water butt had moved from being abandoned behind our shed to upside down in the side passage. It followed my discovery that the world gets through eighty-six million barrels of oil each day. I was so shocked by this that I decided I must do something to help, and the line I took was to offer to speak in school assemblies. Most schools gather their young people once a week in their different year groups, and it is nice for them if a visiting speaker comes from time to time. The talk should be six or seven minutes, no more, and be lively and interesting. I enjoyed the challenge!

The water butt used to come along as my visual aid. It so happened that it was exactly fifty centimetres wide and held fifty gallons. I did the Maths, and calculated that the world's use of oil in just one day would require a line of water butts stretching three quarters of the way round the globe. I have spoken in about fifteen school assemblies to date, and whatever else I said, I always started with the point about the line of water butts. On the whole, the talks were appreciated.

I used to keep the butt upside down so that there wouldn't be a mammoth job cleaning it out each time I needed it for a talk. Now it had a different role, to be used for its original purpose.

The butt is itself made of oil, I reckon, so consuming oil is not only about fuel. I was astonished to discover that fertilisers and pesticides are made from oil and natural gas (I forget which comes from which), and many other products in daily use also come from oil, such as antibiotics. The world could not afford to run short of oil, it seemed to me. It won't now, at any rate.

Sorry, I digress.

As you may imagine, I made an effort after that to communicate the idea of catching rainwater whenever I spent time with the Scullery queue. I visited the roof repairs man of 30 Lambourne Drive and shared my idea with him. Whether people took action or not was up to them. So far, the water pressure had remained constant, but I had no confidence that this would always be the case. Who was going to repair any serious leak if one occurred under the road, for example, and how?

I hope you feel I have given you a reasonable snapshot of what life was like in those days. It is now time to move towards the dramatic events that would shortly unfold.

Chapter Eleven

Hardly a day passed without more immigrants arriving, as we called them. Our community was changing before our eyes. Some were only passing through, being on their way to 'the country', but others wanted to stay. I insisted that our job was to make them all welcome. Indeed, we needed their skills as they needed ours.

I suppose my game plan was to maintain a spirit of co-operation. If it could be well-established in our road, who knows, perhaps it might spread to the neighbourhood, and even further.

Once we started fighting and trying to grab for ourselves, we were lost, I reckoned. However, it was no good being unrealistic. We clearly needed a strategy for dealing with armed gangs entering the area with a view to taking over.

One way of doing this would have been to arm ourselves to the hilt so that we were stronger than all comers. This idea was not so ludicrous as it sounds. There must be plenty of munitions where Mark had done the clay pigeon shooting. Sonia and I would often hear the pop pop of guns to the West in the old days when we would take Timber for a walk out on the heath.

Then we could have been even more ambitious. There were army encampments not that many miles off, and perhaps we could have purloined a pre-microchip armoured car or even a tank (some hope, people scoffed).

These ideas had flitted through my mind in the first few days of The Crisis. If we were going to go down that path, then the sooner we started arming ourselves the better. But I dismissed the thought as soon as it came.

No, instead of an arms race, we needed a peace race. There is another way, I had found myself thinking for some months, there is another way. After all, believing as I did that God made the universe and us within it, why did humanity have to be at daggers drawn with each other? Why not try friendship for a change? Perhaps it might even work!

You will probably think my attitude was incredibly naïve, but I decided I would rather die in the attempt to preserve the peace than take up arms against my fellow man.

It was a job to persuade the others, but I was determined.

"Look," I said firmly to Kath and Phil and Greg, "This is the arrangement. When the armed gang approaches, everybody gets indoors and keeps out of sight to provide no threat. I will strip to my underpants and stand in the middle of the road and welcome them to the town. Nobody is going to shoot a totally defenceless man without parleying. After all, even the most desperate people actually want to get to a place of peace and security in the end, and if they can do it without firing a shot, then so much the better."

They all said I was nuts, but I insisted. "I am the Co-ordinator and that's that," I told them. Rather to my surprise they accepted it without a struggle.

It was not so easy explaining my decision to Mark, but in the end he understood. The result was that I said all my goodbyes in advance, as it were, so that nobody would feel there were any loose ends if a gang did come and chose to eliminate me.

I felt entirely comfortable taking this line because of another memorable sermon from my church-going days. It is curious how some of these buried memories have been stirred up by the recent events. I haven't been to church for years, but I do read the Bible and pray each morning, although not many people know that. I am still a believer at heart.

The sermon had been about the crossing of the River Jordan in Joshua chapter three; I even remember the reference. The bit which caught my attention was that when Joshua commanded, and the waters stood up like a heap so that the people could walk across on the river bed, the first people in were the priests carrying the Ark of the Covenant. They were to stand in the middle of the river while all the people walked past them and out the other side. There were so many folk that the crossing lasted several hours. Think of all that weight of water ready to crash down on them all that time.

The preacher's point was a simple one. "Notice that the true leader puts himself in the most vulnerable place, even the place of most danger, on behalf of those he leads," he proclaimed, or words to that effect.

I loved that. How much better than all the self-seeking and nest-feathering we have seen from so many of our leaders in recent years! No wonder we are in a state.

So the decision to stand in the middle of the road was an easy one for me. Let justice flow like rivers, and righteousness as an ever flowing stream, as another old Testament passage says. In taking the path of peace we had right on our side, a wall of water at our back to crush any opposition as it were. Not that I tried to explain any of this to the others, you understand. It was easier to let them think I was crazy!

Anyway, we have now come to where this account began, as you will have grasped. Greg Phil and I were discussing with some new arrivals whether the radiation from the sun had been earth penetrating, in which case we were fortunate in getting it in the night rather than when the roads and skies were busy, or earth opaque as it were, in which case each country would have been hit at sunrise, when the dreaded shout came.

There I was waiting in the road half naked for I did not know what when a friendly voice rang out, "Matthew!"

I looked up. "Ben," I yelled in delight. This was great. We soon hugged.

"What on earth are you doing out in the middle of the road practically starkers?" Ben enquired.

"Long story," I replied. "I knew you'd turn up sooner or later, but I never expected it would be like this. Who are all these young people with you?"

"Oh, that's SPASM, Jasmine's Church Youth Group. As soon as she heard I was coming into town, she insisted I needed an escort, so they came along in support."

"Spasm?" I asked.

"It stands for Scripture, Prayer And Snack Meeting."

"Naturally."

Ben and I have been friends for years. Jasmine is someone he knows from Badminton; I had met her once or twice. He was soon inside having a cup of tea with me (now fully clothed again). The young people went off into the town, waving their football supporter's rattle and brandishing their length of drainpipe which I had thought was a mortar as they went.

Ben is a Buddhist; however, he is not a full Buddhist Buddhist if you know what I mean. Rather, he appreciates the meditation and calm and reflective side of things. He feels at home in a Quaker Meeting House. I hope you get the drift.

He also enjoys winding me up if I let him. But of course, our present predicament was too important for anything like that.

"How did you know I'd be turning up then?" Ben asked.

"Easy. Prevailing wind."

"Oh yes?"

"Hasn't it become a bit smelly over your way? Sort of whiff in the air?"

"Yes, it's quite unpleasant, but how did you know?"

"I was afraid of it. Ben, I'm pleased to inform you that I have a job for you to do." I took on a magisterial tone. "In fact it's promotion. It requires fortitude, resource, inventiveness and above all," here I flourished a clenched fist in the air for added effect, "a determination to see the job through."

"Yes, but what is it?"

"The sewage farm needs a visit. We can't shy away from it any longer."

"What sewage farm?"

"Our one, here in Starcross. It's on the edge of the meadows beyond us and your village, and as there has been a West wind since The Crisis struck, you must have been receiving the full force of any smell from it."

"Well, thanks very much, and love you too and all that, but what do you think is happening there then?"

"Pretty much nothing, I reckon. Those rotating arms that drizzle water onto beds of pebbles have probably stopped since the power went down for example, and the whole thing will be seizing up."

"I see, and I'm to sort it out. I can hardly wait. Do I get any pay?"

"We'll come up with an appropriate package. No, seriously, somebody needs to investigate. I have been putting it off, but I decided that if the smell got strong enough to drive you over here, then we needed to act."

"Great. So now I'm a sewage farm monitor to add to my other roles. But surely, when they get the power back on is the time to sort it. We can hardly turn those water spraying arms by hand."

"I don't think the power will come back on, not for a long while." I explained to Ben my view about the Sun having knocked out the Silicon chips.

His response was instant.

"Nonsense!" he declared roundly. "It's all the work of terrorists. Why go inventing crazy stories about the sun being involved?"

"How can terrorists be responsible for everything? Not just power off, but computers down, cars disabled, planes grounded, you name it if it's electrical then it's kaput."

"Oh I agree, they have got their act together in a phenomenally successful way, but they have probably been preparing for years. Bring Western democracy to its knees. Anyway, how can the sun affect computer chips?"

"I saw it on TV." I was feeling somewhat defensive by now.

"Right. Pure science, then. Sure it wasn't broadcast on April the first?"

It was a shocking thought. Had I been taken in by a spoof programme? Maybe it was all the work of terrorists after all. Had I caused three needless suicides by rushing to a hasty conclusion?

It had been so hard. At the first meetings, I had not said enough to get them worried, but then later, when I upped the volume as it were, a couple reacted by killing themselves because of what I have said. How could I have got the balance right?

Then I remembered the radio silence; we had said we were going to tune in regularly to Radio Hindhead, and it had gone clean out of my mind.

I told Ben about the silence.

"Well, radio blackout is explained by the power being down it seems to me."

"All over the globe?" I queried.

"If I was in government, and there was a major incident in the Middle East for example, involving oil, or a key gas pipeline being blown up, then I would see to it that any electricity we did have was preserved for vital functions. Radio for the masses hardly counts as vital."

"Well, I hope you're right, but I believe you're wrong. And I wouldn't expect anything from government if I was you. Round here, it's only the farmers, God bless 'em and Bob the policeman who have stayed at their posts, and Bob is a bachelor with no family to consider. We're on our own, Ben. At least we can be grateful that the world is burning less energy and giving the planet a chance to breathe."

Ben is familiar with my views on the environment.

"Another thing. Wouldn't we have noticed a solar flare like that?" he put in.

"Not necessarily. Or rather, perhaps some of the scientists and astronomers did notice but they couldn't communicate with the rest of us. But I reckon the lay man might not be aware of anything. Do you remember that X rays are so-called because when they were discovered around 1900, people just could not believe that anything could go right through the earth? So they called them X Rays as meaning mysterious, incomprehensible. It's a helpful attitude. There's a lot we don't know about radiation. I wouldn't rule out a flare from the sun too speedily."

"Hmm. About all those computers being down saving energy... Matthew, have you any idea how little power a computer actually uses?"

"Well, it's not nothing, and there are so many machines now. Have you heard of this cloud computing they talk about? It requires enormous warehouses the size of many football pitches full of servers, all kept cool by air conditioning. Why, we have one here in Starcross which uses fifty diesel generators apparently; that's three times as much energy as is used by the rest of Starcross put together."

The words were barely out of my mouth when I realised the implications of what I had said.

"Ben!" I cried, standing up. "Come on. There's no time to waste."

But at that very moment there was a loud hammering on our front door. Ben and I covered the ground quickly, and when I opened it, there was Fliss, my lovely daughter covered in mud, her clothes torn and her face severely bruised standing on the doorstep. She took one look at us and burst into tears.

Chapter Twelve

I threw my arms round Fliss and attempted to comfort her, but the girl was so worked up that this was clearly going to take a while.

"You see to Ben," I indicated with a head movement to Mark, who had just joined us, and took Fliss off upstairs.

Fliss was so tearful that she could hardly speak. I washed her face with cold water as best I could and then she took herself off to bed. All I could gather was that she was fundamentally OK but her bike had been stolen and she had been on foot for the last day. It was a remarkable achievement to have made it home at all, it seemed to me.

Pretty soon she was deep in sleep. It was the best thing for her, I reckoned.

This left me in an awkward position. Should I hang around here for who knew how long when it might then prove possible to talk to Fliss, or should we go? She might wake in the next hour, but I doubted it. I reckoned there might be time for both if we were quick...

I made a decision.

"Fliss is out for the count and I have a sense of urgency," I explained to Ben and Mark downstairs in the hall. "Come on, Ben."

"Where?"

"To the generators. Diesel hunt. Mark, there's no need to hang around. She'll sleep the clock round I guess. We'll try not to be too long."

Ben did not argue. In a couple of minutes he and I were both on bikes; Ben borrowed Sonia's. I was sure she would not have minded. We hared off down the road.

It took ten minutes to get to the Industrial Estate. The long road had many units either side of it, and I had never actually been along it before. I only knew it was the location of the data park (for want of a better term) from the local paper.

We rode up and down. It was not obvious which building would be the one we were looking for. Most of them had boards up with the name of their business, but there was one with a well fortified gate and a high fence with security cameras on top that had no name outside.

"I bet this is it," I said.

"How are we going to get in?" Ben enquired.

We walked up and down.

"I think a four metre ladder would get us up and over this fence," I proposed. "All those cameras will be dead, clearly. I wonder where we can get a ladder?"

The quickest way seemed to be to ask a local household. We made our way back out of the Industrial Estate and turned into the first residential road we saw. I knocked on the door of the first house. There was no reply.

A middle aged man spotted us from next door.

"They're in Germany," he called.

"We need to borrow a ladder," I explained.

"You're the hog roast man, aren't you?" The man was coming over. "Great job you fellows are doing.

87

We love it over there. Yes, help yourself to our ladder. Do you need just the one or both?"

He seemed very helpful and was clearly strong. I had an inspiration. "Look, are you free to come with us?" I explained our mission. The man was only too keen to help.

"I'm Malcolm" he explained as the three of us walked along carrying the ladders and wheeling the two bikes.

"I think I could manage these ladders on my bike," said Ben gallantly. He was a good friend; he knew I needed to be there when Fliss woke, so he wanted us not to dawdle. Malcolm was soon on his bike, and the three of us pedalled forwards. Ben was remarkably skilled at riding with two ladders over his left shoulder to weigh him down. I would not have been any good at it at all.

"Sensational!" I breathed. "You should have been in a circus."

Having Malcolm with us made all the difference. We soon had one ladder up on the outside. The fence was very solid, thankfully. Ben shinned up it. Malcolm and I passed up the other ladder just beside him, and he was able to angle it over the top of the fence until it slumped down on the ground the far side. Somehow he kept hold of it in the process, otherwise we might have lost it. We now had an easy up and down route to get into the complex.

"This is better than breaking open the gate," I remarked as we gathered at the foot of the ladder inside.

It was obvious which way to go as there was only one door.

"Looks like we'll have to break this one," Malcolm observed.

I tried the handle without success. I pushed on the door, which gave a little.

All at once there was a deafening sound of a klaxon going off somewhere nearby. It gave a very loud note once a second, more like a loud snort than a note really. I felt so guilty. Here we were, breaking and entering private property. But it was in a good cause. The stock of diesel here could transform things.

"They've got power, then," Malcolm shouted above the din.

Instantly I saw red.

"The generators!" I yelled. "Don't you see? They've not been switched off."

I was past caring. I shot back to the ladder we had just descended, seized it bodily and advanced on the door.

"Help me!" I cried.

We swung it to and fro like a battering ram. All the time the klaxon sounded accusingly in our ears. After weeks without any amplified sound, the effect of it was all the more deafening.

"Don't worry, there's nobody to hear," I yelled. All the same, the three of us looked round nervously as if some second world war combat group was about to charge round a corner and gun us down.

"Keep at it!" I urged. We redoubled our efforts, and sure enough, the doors began to give. One final batter and they flew apart. A blast of cold air hit us in the face.

"This is awful," I called, charging in. It was bitterly cold. We ran forward along a corridor. Lights were switching on all over the place, presumably triggered by our presence.

We burst through a set of swing doors and an extraordinary sight met our eyes. We were on the top catwalk of a huge warehouse filled with computers piled up in racks. There were thick black power cables like snakes running everywhere, all neatly secured with plastic ties. The building was the area of a DIY superstore, and I could tell by the echoing sound of our feet on the grating that there were many floors below us.

We all moved our heads to get a clear view down. There were no solid floors, only grating to permit the circulation of air, allowing us to see. Each successive floor going down appeared identical. The only floor lit was our own, so we could not see all the way down into the murk. The place was freezing cold and there was a steady up draught with an odd smell.

It was a little like looking down from the ceiling of an old cathedral I once visited. I remember climbing up a spiral staircase which led up to the roof, only this one was unusual in having a medieval slit window at every twist of the stair, allowing you to look down into the dimness of the nave below. I imagined each turn of the stair would be the last before we passed above the lofty ceiling, but no, there always seemed to be another gyration until finally the route twisted back on itself and passed through a doorway and we found ourselves out on the leads in the bright sunshine. The contrast between the dim interior and the brightness outside had been noteworthy, more so than the view we had climbed up to see, in my opinion.

Just for a wild moment, I wondered if there really was a bottom to the warehouse. Perhaps the enormous stack of computers went right on down on floor after floor to the centre of the earth and out the other side and on across the universe...

My instinct was to step back from the up-welling cold air in case any foreign body was blown up from the depths and went in my eye.

"Each machine is powered up, you notice," Ben's loud voice above the noise interrupting my thoughts sounded strange, "because their power lights are on, but there are none of the winking lights you might expect from computers in operation."

This was true. The lights going all the way down looked like the unblinking eyes of nocturnal animals studying us intently in the dark, stuck in a time warp. If the flow of time revived, might they rise up at speed on the up draught to attack us, I wondered?

Malcolm was less fazed than the rest of us. "The generators must be through that door," he pointed. There was a way out on the far side.

I remembered the urgency. We charged across the vast pit on one of the many catwalks, our feet making a clanging sound which echoed. The distant rumble grew steadily louder as we did so, and when we made our way through two sets of double swing doors, there were the powerful cast iron generators in front of us, letting out a continuous bellow. The temperature was much higher in here.

Even as we stood there, one of the huge machines coughed a few times and died.

"Quick, let's switch them off!" I urged.

Thankfully this was not difficult. Each one had a box with red and green buttons on it, and a sharp blow to the red button with the palm caused the thundering and vibrating to stop. I worked my way to the left along the row. After just three or four machines, I found some that were already still. In fact the rest of them in my direction were all still. Fear seized my insides.

The building was soon eerily silent. I rejoined the others.

"How many did you switch off?" I asked Ben.

"Six," he replied.

"Four," Malcolm volunteered. I had done four as well.

"That makes just fourteen still running," I observed in a small voice, "in other words, thirty-six have already run out of fuel. This power house has been burning up valuable diesel keeping non-functioning computers cold ever since The Crisis began. To think of it; we have had a mammoth freezer in our midst which could have been preserving food, consuming precious fuel, pouring out carbon dioxide into the bargain, all to no purpose whatever!"

I suppose that part of me deep down had already been prepared for this situation, for the diesel still being burnt pointlessly. You could rely on people to be irresponsible, it seemed to me. All the same, I felt a great surge of anger. Suddenly, all the pent up emotion of the last few weeks rose up in my throat. I let out a great cry.

"Surely somebody must have known about this! Couldn't someone have come and turned these monsters off?"

I don't think I have ever been so upset. It took the others several minutes to calm me down, by which time we had gone back through to the outside. The klaxon had stopped, but I barely noticed. I was feeling absolutely wrung out.

There would be some diesel left to harvest but only a fraction of what we might have had. It was heart-breaking.

We closed the battered door as best we could, put the ladder back up and climbed back over the fence.

"We haven't time to do any more now," Ben urged. "You need to be there for Fliss."

It was true. Malcolm had been terrific, and I told him so, somehow. He and Ben took the ladders back between them so that I could cycle on home with the least delay. It is the only time in my life that I have ever ridden through the streets with the tears pouring down my face, but what did it matter what anybody thought? I was past caring.

Chapter Thirteen

Kath was there in the hall when I came in. I was clearly in disgrace.

"Fliss is asleep in bed. Mark went off with the horse and cart an hour ago because you had taken his bicycle without asking. He was looking like thunder. I won't ask what you were doing that was so important."

I sighed. Actually it was my bike, but don't raise that issue.

I recalled my first day at Primary School. My mother had sent me in a pair of dungarees which I had never worn before, and when it came to the moment to visit the toilets, I did not know how to undo them. None of the girls helped me (we little ones used the girls toilets for the first few weeks, presumably to protect us from the horrid boys which we would ourselves one day become). By the time I had managed the task and returned to the classroom, I was last by a long way. "You're in disgrace!" hissed a girl beside me as I sat down, which sounded very threatening, but as the teacher never referred to it, nor anybody else for that matter, to this day I don't know what being in disgrace meant in practice. Indeed, in many ways, I feel I have been in disgrace ever since.

"How did you know Fliss had come home?" I asked simply.

"Mark told me. He seems to have everything in hand. She's lost her bike but that's all, thank goodness, but it was a close thing. It's taken her days to get here. She rode all day and tried to find a place to sleep at night. The first two outhouses she selected were alright, but the hay barn she tried on the third night was nearly her undoing. She could hear someone moving about in the dark. She stayed still, petrified, and thankfully he didn't find her, but in the morning her bike had gone. The sensible girl had hidden it a few hundred yards away from her hidy-hole so as not to attract attention. Thankfully she was not too far from home by then and was able to walk the rest of the way. She's worn out, but she'll be OK. It's wonderful that she's got back in one piece."

I felt troubled by this turn of events. Mark must have woken Fliss after I had gone out and extracted all this information from her. Now here I was being told of our intimate family affairs by our next door neighbour. Why couldn't Mark have left his sister to sleep?

I also felt very uneasy at the story. I have never known Fliss to lie, but I was left with questions; if there had been no attack, how had she come by the torn clothes and all that bruising?

"And Mark?" I enquired gently. "Did he say where he was going?"

"No, but I think he's gone to look for her bike."

Oh dear. I thanked Kath for her concern, made an excuse and went to the place where I had hidden my shotgun. It was missing. This was grim. I thought I had chosen a secure place, and that nobody but me would have thought to look for it there, but I suppose that was wishful thinking.

Mark was better off in the cart than on my bike, I reckoned, because if he did discover her bike, he could sling it in the back. But was that all there was to it? He had seen Fliss in the state she was in on arrival. Had he drawn his own conclusions and gone charging off with another agenda than what he had told Kath?

In short, was I busily trying to save the community and all the time my own family was spiralling downwards into violence in front of my own eyes?

I felt both uneasy and powerless. I just had to hope he would not do anything foolish. I wish he had never got hold of that gun.

Kath was still there when I returned to the hall. I thanked her very much for staying.

"She may need some feminine attention later," I found myself saying, perhaps unwisely. "May I call you?"

Kath nodded as she made her way back next door. It occurred to me as she was leaving that Pamela would know better what to do. I had been so wrong about her and the Community Hospital. What a fool I was!

Ben was back within a few minutes. We had a late lunch; soup from the Scullery, then yet another cold salad with things from the garden, and then soup again as a dessert. As long as you left an hour's interval between servings of soup, the flavour and consistency were guaranteed to be different the second time round.

Ben was very impressed with the Scullery. "Well, I can see you're pretty well organised here, but what do you want this crystal cathedral for?"

I had shown him the huge piles of bottles and jars upstairs, some of which were perched precariously.

"Bottling fruit. You boil it up furiously, and then put it into sterilised jars. Jam-making would have been nice, but there's already a shortage of sugar so it's out of the question."

There was still no seeing Fliss, it seemed. Ben and I were soon sitting in the garden, with a cup of tea made with hot water from a thermos flask. There was a permanent kettle on top of a wood-burning stove in a house a few doors away, and all the local houses filled thermoses from it. Or should that be thermoi perhaps?

It was good that people had gone in for wood burning stoves in recent years, with oil and gas prices beginning to rise, although some people had fitted ones which went in the wall and therefore had no surface on top where you could boil up. This now appeared short-sighted. Finding enough logs to burn was going to become an issue before long, I reckoned.

"Have you seen our apples?" I pointed to our new 'family' apple tree, three different varieties grafted onto one root stock. "In the first year of a new tree, you cut off all the little apples that form so that the tree puts all its energy into growing strong. However, I missed two down near the bottom and now they have swelled up. Don't they look great?"

"Yes indeed. When are you going to pick them?"

"How about wait for one to drop and then pick and eat the second? That's what you do with a brace of grouse hanging in the game larder, apparently."

"Rather a waste, I'd have thought," said Ben, "But look, back to the subject. For the sake of argument, just suppose you're right in your view that the world's computer chips are now useless. Where does that leave us?"

"Up a creek without a paddle. Nothing works any more, and it will take decades if not centuries to fix it all."

"Right. How enticing."

"Some things will never be fixed. Take a Sat Nav, for example. Not only is the chip inside the console useless, the satellite it communicates with will have been knocked out too. To replace them will need rockets, and the electronic wizardry to get those up into space will all have to be built from scratch. By the time that's done, the world will have moved on, and we might not even have private cars anyhow."

"All those communications satellites are finished, I suppose. Weather forecasting is back to licking your finger and putting it in the air for the time being!"

"All our systems have broken down, because we did not realise that computer chips have an Achilles heal. But that only applies to the countries we have thought of as advanced. In Africa, things will be carrying on pretty much as normal, I reckon."

"Fascinating. 'The first shall be last, and the last first.'"

Ben likes talking religion with me. We have learned to respect each other's different opinions.

It's a matter of not getting too worked up in our discussions.

"We thought we were on solid ground," I observed, "but really what we were putting so much weight on was paper thin."

"Matthew, if what you're saying is right, and we are in for a long haul lasting several lifetimes, then according to your philosophy, there will be something about it in the Bible. I bet you've thought about that."

"Yes, I have actually. I found myself reflecting on the four horsemen of the apocalypse, in the book of Revelation. The first one is victory, then the second one is war, number three is famine and number four is death."

"Charming."

"Well, perhaps. But the sequence is interesting. First of all you get conquest – man thinking he is so clever that he can do anything and is master of the universe. You know the sort of thing. But then when times get difficult, conflict arises. In an extreme situation that leads to price rises and food shortages, and death is not far behind. So yes, I can see similarities with our present predicament. We all thought we were so clever with our little hand-held devices, but in fact in moving forward, we were putting our heads into a noose we were not aware of, and now it's beginning to draw tight."

"What a frightening image. How many people are going to die, then, according to the good book?"

I glanced at his face. It had been a gibe, but I ignored it.

"In one place in Revelation it says a quarter of the population, but in another place it says a third."

"God!"

"But that's not all," I persisted. "As I say, we in the West are stuffed, but Africa and non-computerised rural communities generally will pull through, as they have not committed themselves to the new technology in the same way as us, so the death toll is likely to be much higher in our country than over there."

It was shocking, I had to admit.

Chapter Fourteen

I ought to explain that Ben and I met fifteen years ago and have been friends ever since. We have tended to meet to watch a film on a Friday evening when Sonia was generally out. Or used to meet before our present troubles, I should have said.

He took a moment or two to digest what I had said. Then he spoke.

"When I was at school, I seem to recall the RE teacher saying that people had interpreted the Black Death of the middle ages as fulfilling the prophecies in Revelation. A third of the population across Europe died. People created pictures of the grim reaper along with those four horsemen you spoke of. So perhaps the prophecy has been fulfilled already and that's that."

Ben is no fool. It was a wonderful statement, I thought.

"Well, you may be right. But personally I don't understand prophecy that way. Scripture says 'The word of the Lord lasts for ever.' If you like, think of the game Ducks and Drakes, spinning a flat stone as you throw it on the surface of a lake so that it bounces a few times before falling in. You know what I'm talking about?"

"Go on."

"I see biblical prophecy in the same way, as having a permanent energy like the spinning stone, touching down in history not one time but many times. Otherwise why bother to read the Bible at all today? People do it because they believe it remains valid from one generation to the next."

"It could all be bogus."

"Oh yes, I agree. But that's a decision we all have to make."

I decided to be a little mischievous.

"To me, the prophecies in Isaiah, Jeremiah and Ezekiel about the people returning to the land of Israel after the exile are a good example. People thought they had been fulfilled in 538BC when the exiles returned from Babylon to their homeland, but I also see a fulfilment in 1948 with the creation of the modern state of Israel and the right of return of Jews to their land. I have a mental image of skimming a stone hard into the water near the edge of the lake so that it rises up in a long arc before plunging down again a hundred metres out from the shore."

"Hmm. Not a very popular view in certain quarters."

"No, granted. We can have a go at that issue some other time if we want! I was only trying to explain that prophecy is not exhausted by a single application."

"Right. So you think world population could decrease by a third as a result of this crisis, with most deaths in the developed world."

"Well, it sounds rather stark put like that, and I wouldn't want to voice my opinion to most people, but yes, that is what I think. And the thing which really worries me is what is going to happen next winter. Supposing there are a lot of deaths? Do we fill up the railway cutting out of town with dead bodies and cover them over? Seems a bit tough on the railway people when they want to re-open the line, with a steam train perhaps. Or do we select a field in the country and just lay the bodies on the ground and let the animals and birds take over? We could even set traps and catch ourselves some food to eat; at least that way we would be avoiding cannibalism."

"Oh Matthew." Ben covered his face with his hands. "How frightful. You're way ahead of me there. Frankly I have no idea. But why are you so sure there will be severe food shortages?"

"It's all this last minute stuff. 'Just In Time' they call it. The big grocery chains have decided that food standing on shelves in warehouses costs money, and the smart thing to do is to be so up to date with what the customers are buying that the supplies can go straight into the stores rather than into warehouses. The computers have made this possible. But the result of that is that now things have collapsed, there will be very little food in storage. The looters will find that there is precious little to loot. We depend on imports for a large chunk of our food, and they aren't going to be resumed in a hurry, so I predict mass starvation. Sorry to be so gloomy, but I daren't talk about these things to anybody other than you, and it's a relief to be able to verbalise them."

There was another pause while we both considered what we were discussing. I became aware that the afternoon was not as warm as it had been; dark clouds were beginning to come over. Still, I did not want to propose moving indoors, as we were having a good conversation and it might get cut off.

It was time for something a bit lighter.

"I wonder what will happen about the Space Elevator?" I enquired, with a twinkle in my eye.

"Go on!" said Ben, with a resigned tone, but obviously ready to be amused by what I would say.

"It's a cheap way to get into space. All you need is a cable fifty-five thousand miles long..."

"All!"

"...Fifty-five thousand miles long going up from the surface of the earth to an appropriate weight of some kind at the top to keep the thing taut by centrifugal force, a small asteroid for example, and then little robot cabins can haul themselves up it to get into orbit."

"Just like that."

I pressed on. "You have to build it from the geostationary orbit in both directions at the same time, up and down, so that the centre of gravity stays on the geostationary orbit, or it would all come tumbling down. The difficulty is making a cable strong enough to withstand the great strain placed on it, which is largest at the point of the geostationary orbit."

"Naturally. You and your science fiction." Ben was enjoying this.

"Science fiction has a way of becoming science fact, Ben. The view used to be that a space elevator could not be built for three hundred years, but with the arrival of immensely strong materials, namely

Carbon Nanotubes, there are people who reckon it might be possible within a decade or two."

"Right. You realise there is another difficulty?"

"Oh?"

"Little nasties might decide to come down the elevator as well as up, namely aliens."

"Very funny. Well, after you have sorted out the sewage plant, you can be officer in charge of fending off what comes down from above" I quipped. "You can borrow my umbrella."

It wasn't a joke I could have made with many people, but Ben found it funny.

"No, seriously," I continued. "The only way forward for the human race is to expand into space. It is only a matter of time before we run out of materials on the earth's surface, but there is no shortage of them up there. We can mine the asteroids for example, and capture solar energy in orbiting power stations, reducing pollution down here. But getting into orbit by rocket is terribly expensive, and the space elevator is the best candidate for getting the cost down. There's even the possibility of taking water from the ocean off our planet to the moon, which would make a great resource for the colonists there as well as helping to counter sea level rise here."

"Matthew, I love your enthusiasm! It's such fun."

"And if you when you've travelled up from the surface of the earth you let go at the top of the cable, you already have escape velocity and can get to anywhere in the solar system."

"I can't wait!"

"And there's even a hint of us expanding to the stars in the Bible," I added. I was really enjoying this.

"Oh yes? Where?"

"Aha!" I said with a chuckle. It would be a mistake to give that one away too easily.

"I suppose it's the issue I feel saddest about in all this, really. Creating the first space elevator has just been put on hold indefinitely, it seems to me. It's such a shame we didn't get on with it while we had the technology and the resources had not yet run down. That was the danger as I saw it, that we frittered away all the fossil fuels on unimportant things for our own pleasures, as if there was an inexhaustible supply, only to wake up with a severe hangover one day. Although I suppose you could say that the hangover has already happened and it's what we've got now."

"I'm dubious about the sea level rising," Ben declared. "Think how vast the surface area of the oceans is. The idea of a few melting glaciers affecting the sea level seriously is somewhat ridiculous to my mind."

"I agree it's hard to imagine. Also it is too slow to observe – six centimetres a decade they say."

I clenched my four fingers hiding my thumb behind them to demonstrate six centimetres.

"But Ben, the trouble is that it's relentless. Even though we have now stopped burning carbon, which is one good result of our present problems, the sea level will still go on rising for centuries until the whole system reaches equilibrium, as I understand it. And they think that up to a billion people live within a metre of sea level. It's a huge problem. We cannot afford to be complacent."

I changed tack again.

"You realise that banking and securities, stocks and shares, all that kind of thing where money changes hands electronically, is finished?"

Ben thought for a moment, then clapped his hands in glee.

"So the Zimbabwean Dollar is now the world's most stable currency I suppose! What a delicious irony!"

We both laughed aloud.

"We are continuing to use the cash in our pockets here in Starcross," I said. "I even wondered whether we could reintroduce some of the old coins as higher denominations."

"Don't tell me! You want to use your old pennies from before 1970 as fifty pound coins. What a great notion."

I had showed Ben my collection of old pennies once before. The proper size ones, not today's minute affairs.

"Did I ever tell you about my best moment?" I asked. "It was when I was seven or eight and the family were at the seaside - Barry Island in South Wales - for the day. I used to enjoy the amusement arcades in those days, and my parents would give me five shillings which I would turn into sixty pennies at the change booth and then have a happy hour before I lost it all. Only before starting, I would look through and take out any Victorian pennies to keep.

"You remember that in our youth, the earliest pennies dated from 1860. Well I can still remember now my joy when I was playing some fruit machine or other and out came an 1869 coin. There were three or four Victorian coins in my book which were described as rare, but 1869 was the only one which was said to be very rare, and I had never seen one before. I gave a shout of delight. The other children thought I was nuts!"

"Some of us still wonder that at times!" Ben said with a twinkle in his eye.

"I think I've still got it somewhere, but I'm rather concerned as it's not with the others. I think I may have hidden it somewhere safe as being extra precious. I only hope it hasn't got lost in the process. I wouldn't put it past my Mum to have thrown it out years ago. She was a great one for throwing precious things out."

"You know, you are extraordinary, Matthew. One minute you can be calmly saying that most of the inhabitants of our country are going to die, and the next you are going on about an outdated coin that is of no earthly use to anybody!"

I laughed. "You're right. I suppose we shouldn't be too hard on all the boffins and whiz kids who got us into this mess with all their computerisation of society. They just got caught up in the enthusiasm for it all. The products were fabulous, after all. It only goes to show that it is possible to be both clever and unwise at the same time. Have another cup of tea."

Ben accepted. The sky really was getting darker now, and the remaining water in the flask was tepid rather than hot, and a tea bag on its ninth use has to be described as a disappointment, and some milk in the tea would have been nice, and Ben was using up the last of our sugar although he didn't know it, but still it was good to be talking together here. I felt happier than I had done in ages.

"Look, I'm sorry; I've been doing all the talking. How have you getting on in your neck of the woods?" I enquired.

"I thought you were never going to ask."

"I apologise. I have been so wound up over events here."

"That's OK. But before we get onto all that, just suppose you're right about the computer chips being over-cooked. There is a way we could get out of this mess."

I stiffened. "How?" This was important.

"What you have to understand…"

I held up my hand to silence him. We were quiet for a moment, and then there it was again, gunfire from the far end of our road. Ben heard it too this time.

"Here we go again!" I said. "Twice in one day!"

I sounded jocular, but fear was already gripping my insides.

"Don't trouble anybody else," I said, as I began to remove my clothes. It was getting very dark, and the wind was getting up. We were in for a storm. A few spots of rain began to fall.

"Look, don't you think…?"

I silenced Ben again.

"Please don't try to stop me. The only chance for us all is if we can pull together, and I have decided on this proactive non-aggressive approach. If it fails, it fails." Then in an afterthought, I added, "You will look after my children if it goes wrong?"

Ben nodded. He was unable to find any words.

"It's been great being friends!" I said hurriedly, as I hugged him. There was no time for more.

I raced down the side passage in my underpants and sandals, slid back the gate, closed it again behind me, and took up my position in the middle of the road. It was deserted. I shivered. Talk about an English summer! It was freezing.

There was a burst of machine gun fire just round the bend. How could I have been taken in by the earlier football rattle? This was far louder and more menacing.

The day had become so dark that it was hard to see.

I held up both my hands towards them as a sign to halt. They were rounding the corner. They had spotted me. There was another rat-tat-tat-tat, this time hideously close.

I had always imagined that a hail of bullets would be painful, but this was no more than autumn leaves falling on my face and hair, to be swept away with a toss of the head.

Instantly a brilliant white search-light shone full in my face. Everything else went black in contrast. It was glorious!

A strange, piercing joy flooded me. These were not enemies ahead; they were friends! The relief had come. I knew it. Great joy welled up inside me. A huge burden rolled off my shoulders. There was a future and a hope after all! My gesture changed into a friendly wave of greeting. I wanted to dance and sing!

I began to stride forward.

Acknowledgements

Clarke, Arthur C and Baxter, Stephen, *Sunstorm*,
Gollancz, London, 2005, page 247.

Evans, Christopher, *The Mighty Micro*, Gollancz, London,
1979 (title only).

Howell, David and Nakhle, Carole, *Out of the Energy
Labyrinth*, I.B.Tauris, London, 2007, especially pages
66-67.

Kunstler, James H, *The Long Emergency*, Atlantic Books,
London, 2005.

Kunstler, James H, *World Made by Hand*, Atlantic
Monthly Press, New York, 2008.

Lovelock, James, *The Revenge of Gaia*, Penguin, London,
2007, photo opposite page 78.

Martin, James, *The Meaning of the Twenty-first Century*,
Eden Project Books, London, 2007, especially 92-93
and most especially of all, page 241.

Rees, Martin, *Our Final Century*, Heinemann, London,
2003.

Afterword

I became neighbourhood watch co-ordinator for our end of Oriental Road Woking about twenty years ago. There has been nothing to do; indeed, very few residents even know that we have a neighbourhood watch scheme, let alone that I am in charge. When Covid19 struck I tried to get us all to pull together, but only a third of households responded. I try to keep an eye on the elderly and lonely, all of whom have family locally, so there isn't much need. Perhaps this story arose from my desire to have something useful to contribute!

Printed in Great Britain
by Amazon